★

Geena's heart started to pound wildly. This wasn't how it was supposed to happen. The ball was supposed to stay on the Meteors' side of the field. But the Meteors' center attacker dribbled straight for the Stars' goal.

Keep your eye on the ball, she told herself. She bent her knees and tried to stay calm. She was so nervous her knees were quivering.

Playing goalkeeper always made her uptight. But today was worse than usual. Geena knew that each time the Meteors shot on goal, everyone— the ref, Marina, all the parents—would be watching her. What if someone noticed her cast? As if keeping the ball out of the goal wasn't enough to worry about.

The attacker kept coming as steadily as an express train. *This is bad*, Geena thought. *Very, very bad.*

Against
the Rules

Against the Rules

by

Emily Costello

A SKYLARK BOOK

NEW YORK · TORONTO · LONDON · SYDNEY · AUCKLAND

RL 5, 008–012

AGAINST THE RULES

A Bantam Skylark Book/July 1998

Skylark Books is a registered trademark of Bantam Books, a division of Bantam Doubleday Dell Publishing Group, Inc. Registered in U.S. Patent and Trademark Office and elsewhere.

ISBN 0-553-48646-2

Published simultaneously in the United States and Canada

Bantam Books are published by Bantam Books, a division of Bantam Doubleday Dell Publishing Group, Inc. Its trademark, consisting of the words "Bantam Books" and the portrayal of a rooster, is Registered in U.S. Patent and Trademark Office and in other countries. Marca Registrada. Bantam Books, 1540 Broadway, New York, New York 10036.

PRINTED IN THE UNITED STATES OF AMERICA

OPM   0   9   8   7   6   5   4   3   2   1

For Miranda Sage
and Victoria Laurel Nelson

Chapter 1

"SUBSTITUTIONS!" THE REF HOLLERED.

Nicole Philips-Smith and Lacey Essex exchanged amused glances as their teammates trudged toward the sidelines. The Stars' league played short-sided, which meant that nine players max were allowed on the field. Since the team had eleven members, two players always had to sit out. Nicole and Lacey had spent the last twelve and a half minutes cheering for their teammates.

The girls coming off the field were muddy up to their thighs. Midfielder Tameka Thomas, who had taken a spill while running with the ball, even had mud on her shirt and in her hair.

A steady rain had been falling on Beachside

for five days straight. Even though the rain had stopped by Friday night, the sky was still cloudy and the field was a grass-and-mud mess when the Stars arrived for their game against the Galaxy on Saturday afternoon.

Marina Santana, the Stars' coach, was wearing cleats, shorts, and a blue windbreaker. "How's it going out there?" she asked.

Geena Di Gregorio laughed. "It's slippery, but great!"

Nicole shot Geena a give-me-a-break look.

Geena just grinned back.

Nicole and Geena had struck up a friendship when they started playing soccer together that spring. The girls didn't have much in common except soccer. Nicole was the youngest kid in her family. Geena was the oldest in hers. The girls went to different schools, lived in different neighborhoods—sometimes Nicole even thought they lived in different worlds. Geena was so *upbeat* all the time—Nicole didn't get it. Geena never got mad or upset. Her sunny attitude reminded Nicole of her kindergarten teacher: all enthusiasm all the time.

"Marina? Could you take me out?" Rose

O'Connor asked. Her voice was hoarse, and she looked pale. "My throat hurts."

"Sure thing." Marina nodded at Nicole. "Take over for Rose as left attacker. And, Fiona, you can come out too. Lacey, you'll be our center midfielder."

Tameka gave Nicole a sideways hug, wiggling her muddy side against her. "Welcome to the game!"

Nicole glanced down at her now dirty uniform and shook her head at Tameka. "Massively funny."

"Thanks."

"Let's go!" the ref shouted.

Nicole ran onto the field with her teammates, her cleats making sucking sounds in the mud. The girls lined up, and the Galaxy center attacker took the kickoff, passing to her left.

The Galaxy left attacker waited for the ball, which bumped across the rutted field in slo-mo. Tess Adams, the Stars' right attacker, didn't wait. She intercepted the ball and quickly drove forward.

Nicole ran along the touchline, into Galaxy territory. Clumps of mud flew up behind her.

Tess steered the ball straight up the middle of

the field, managing to get close to the Galaxy's goal before two midfielders started putting pressure on her.

"I'm open!" Nicole shouted.

Tess whacked the ball with her left foot. She was aiming at Nicole, but the mud slowed the pass. Nicole put on a burst of speed to meet the ball halfway. She crossed into the middle of the field, splashing right through a puddle.

Nicole had her eyes on the ball, but she could hear someone pounding down the field behind her. One of the Galaxy players. The race was on.

"Get it, Nicole!"

"Go, Nicki, go!"

Nicole raced for the ball, pushing herself to get there first. But the Galaxy player reached out and got a foot on the ball while Nicole was maneuvering into position. Nicole glanced up at her opponent's face—plaster-white skin, icy blue eyes, and long black hair falling in ringlets. Nicole felt a spasm of dislike. She wasn't battling just *any* Galaxy player, she was battling the witch of Country Day Academy. Sheila McGarth.

"Get out of my way, Nicole," Sheila warned.

"In your dreams."

Gritting her teeth, Nicole kicked the ball as hard as she could. But Sheila was kicking from the other side at the same time. Shallow thudding noises came from the ball, but it didn't move. Nicole kicked again and again, occasionally hitting the ball slightly off center and clanking on Sheila's shin guards. Her leg was getting tired. Still the ball didn't budge.

Suddenly Nicole knew what she had to do. Planting her right foot, she brought her left foot back as if she were about to give the ball a solid kick. Instead she waited for Sheila to whack the ball. Nicole intercepted the kick. When she did, she pulled the ball toward her, slowing it down.

Eyes on the nearby goal, Nicole started to dribble. Just as she thought she was free of Sheila, Nicole's right foot jerked out from under her. She went down hard, feeling the muddy ground scrape the skin off one of her knees.

She tripped me, Nicole told herself, only half surprised. Sheila always played to win, and not only on the soccer field. Nicole knew from experience that Sheila didn't mind cheating to get what she wanted.

The ref blew her whistle to signal the call. "Tripping—Galaxy. Since the ball was in the penalty area, the Stars get a penalty kick."

Nicole got to her feet, shot Sheila a poisonous look, and gently brushed the mud from her knees.

"Take it, Nicole!" Marina yelled from the sidelines.

Nicole felt a bit unsure of what to do. The Stars practiced penalty kicks occasionally, but it had been a couple of seasons since she had taken one in a game. The American Youth Soccer Organization league the Stars played in stressed good sportsmanship. Most everyone played clean, and that meant penalty kicks were rare.

The ref made a face as she scooped up the wet, muddy ball. She quickly handed it to Nicole.

Nicole put the ball down on the penalty mark, which was directly in front of the Galaxy goal. She wiped her muddy hands on her shorts.

"Good luck," Tameka said, and gave Nicole a pat on the back.

"The goalkeeper is tiny," Tess whispered. "Try to hit it above her head." She motioned for the rest of the Stars to move out of the penalty area. A kicker's teammates weren't allowed to touch the ball until after the kick.

A hush passed over the field. Players, coaches, moms, and dads—everyone was watching Nicole and the Galaxy goalkeeper. If Nicole could get off a decent shot, the Stars would score and the game would be tied.

As she took her place behind the ball, Nicole stared right into the eyes of the Galaxy goalkeeper, a skinny girl whose stringy hair was falling into her eyes. The goalkeeper looked nervous.

Nicole could relate. She backed up a few feet, rubbing her hands together.

"Don't worry," she heard Sheila say loudly. "Nicole's a loser. She'll miss."

Nicole knew Sheila was trying to ruin her concentration. *Watch this, peahead,* she thought as she ran forward and let the ball have it—a solid instep kick.

She was aiming for the goal's upper left corner. But the mud-encrusted ball was heavier than usual. The ball headed toward the goalkeeper at about waist height.

Great shot, Nicole, she thought sourly. *No way she'll miss that. Be ready.*

The Galaxy goalkeeper grunted as she caught the ball against her stomach. She used both hands to roll it out of the goal.

Nicole sprang forward and kicked the ball again. This time she sent it like a bullet into the net.

"Goal—Stars!" the ref yelled.

Nicole caught Sheila's gaze and held it until Sheila looked away. *Give me your best shot,* Nicole challenged Sheila silently. *I'll give it right back to you.*

"You have mud on your face," Tess told Tameka during halftime. The Stars were hanging out on the side of the field. Usually they spent halftime lounging around under the trees, but nobody wanted to sit in the wet grass.

Tameka reached up and ran a hand over her face. "No, I don't."

Tess flicked a little clump of mud at her friend, hitting her right in the cheek. "Now you do!" she cried, getting ready to run.

But Tameka only rolled her eyes. "Grow up, Adams." She smiled to show she wasn't really angry.

Tess pouted. "I just wanted you to look special. Like the Galaxy players do."

Tameka looked across the field, where the opposing team had huddled around its coaches. She knew that each girl had a tiny spiral galaxy painted on her face, just under her right eye. The spirals looked like cartoons of water swirling down a drain. Tameka had noticed the designs as soon as the Galaxy had arrived.

"No joking—I think those designs look cool," Tameka said.

Tess didn't seem to hear her. "I'm cold," she said. "I hate standing around."

Tameka smiled. The rest of the team loved halftime. The ten-minute break gave them time to socialize—not to mention *rest*, after running all over the field for twenty-five minutes. But Tess wasn't really into rest. She liked to play—play hard and win. Tameka had spent the entire season trying to get her best friend to relax a little.

Tess started running in place to keep warm. She lifted her knees so high that she practically knocked herself in the chin. "Face painting is definitely a great way to show team spirit. I wish we'd thought of it."

Yasmine Madrigal was standing nearby. "We have more team spirit than the Galaxy does."

"I know," Tess said. "I think we should do something to show it."

"We can't paint stars on our faces," Tameka said. "The Galaxy will say we're copying."

Tess was still doing her goofy jog. "Then we'll think of something else."

chapter 2

THE SECOND HALF WAS TWENTY MINUTES OLD when Fiona Fagan got possession of the ball. Out of the corner of her eye, Nicole saw Fiona's father lift his video camera and point it at his daughter.

Fiona was dribbling slowly up the touchline. Sheila was covering Fiona, batting at the ball.

Nicole kept even with Fiona and her shadow, staying close but out of the way. "I'm open," she shouted.

Fiona didn't get a chance to pass. She fell, stumbling sideways, and let the ball roll over the touchline.

"Throw-in—Galaxy!" the ref called.

While a short, tough-looking Galaxy midfielder

got ready to take the throw-in, Nicole heard a shout from the direction of the Stars' goal. She spun around in time to see Sarah Mere come out of the goal and throw a clump of mud at Jordan Goldman. Of course Sarah missed. She had terrible aim.

Amber Chappel tackled Sarah from behind, pulling her down into a lake-sized puddle just in front of the goal.

This is our defense? Nicole thought. The Galaxy could probably drive a ball right into the goal without their noticing.

Nicole glanced toward the sidelines. Marina was chatting with Mr. Thomas, the Stars' assistant coach. She didn't seem concerned that her team's defense was more interested in mud wrestling than soccer.

Well, *Nicole* was concerned. The score was tied. All the Stars needed was one more goal—and then Sheila would learn a little lesson.

"Get in the game, you guys!" Nicole yelled.

Sarah got to her feet, drew herself to attention, and saluted Nicole.

The Galaxy midfielder let the ball fly—throwing it straight to Sheila. She got control and started to dribble toward the Stars' goal. Now Fiona was on *her*.

Nicole glanced quickly at the Stars' defense. Amber, Jordan, and Sarah looked alert. *Good,* Nicole thought. She turned her attention back to the ball, ready to intercept.

Sheila looked toward the Stars' goal, apparently sizing up her chance to score, then took an extra second to smirk at Nicole. Too bad for her. The instant she looked away from the ball, Fiona stole it and turned it around, heading diagonally across the field.

Sheila's face dropped in shock. She charged after Fiona. Catching up, Sheila brought her foot back as if she were shooting on goal. She kicked with all her might—hitting Fiona's right knee just above her shin guard.

Fiona howled. She stopped running, clutching her knee.

Nicole jogged over. "Are you okay?" she asked her teammate.

Fiona's face was contorted with pain, but she nodded.

Only then did Nicole realize that the ball was

still in play. The ref hadn't stopped the game, which had to mean she hadn't noticed Sheila's foul.

So where was the ball? Nicole did a quick 360.

Sheila had it! And she was heading straight toward the Stars' goal. Nicole spotted Sheila just in time to watch her fake out Jordan and slam a powerful shot right past Sarah's outstretched fingers.

"Goal—Galaxy!" the ref shouted.

Nicole stomped her foot. "No fair!" she yelled. Hadn't any of the coaches or parents noticed what Sheila had done?

Apparently not.

The teams lined up again, with Fiona limping into place. Play resumed. Nicole fought hard for the rest of the game. She and Tess managed to work the ball right in front of the Galaxy goal a couple of times. But they never got off a decent shot.

Final score: Galaxy 2, Stars 1.

"Geena! Geena, come quick!"

Geena pulled her jacket the rest of the way over her head. She looked down into the face of Naomi, her seven-year-old sister.

Naomi's hazel eyes were bright with excitement. She was bouncing impatiently from foot to foot. Geena knew the signs: Naomi had a juicy piece of information, and she couldn't wait to spill it.

Geena sighed. Naomi had an uncanny ability to sense whenever anyone was doing something wrong—and find out the details. In a family with seven kids, someone was usually up to something.

When Peter and Marco—two of Geena and Naomi's brothers—hid a baby rabbit in their room, Naomi told. When two-year-old Isabella stole all baby Sophia's pacifiers, Naomi told. She even told when Mr. Di Gregorio snatched an extra cookie when he was supposed to be dieting.

Geena loved Naomi, but living with a spy and a snitch was . . . inconvenient. She'd tried to explain to Naomi why tattling wasn't nice. That hadn't worked, so now Geena was determined to discourage Naomi by refusing to listen to any of her stories.

"Stop," Geena said, holding one hand up like a traffic cop. "Whatever it is, I don't want to hear it."

Naomi rolled her eyes. "Yes, you do," she said with certainty. "Nicole is about to have a fight!"

"Nicole?" That got Geena's attention. "Where?"

"By the bathrooms," Naomi reported. "She told me she was waiting for one of the girls from the Galaxy, and that she was gonna *get* her."

Geena took off at a dead run, Naomi right on her heels.

Okay, so maybe the little squealer has her uses, Geena thought. *Especially since her information is usually correct.* But this sounded incredible. Why would Nicole want to beat someone up? She was more the type to get revenge by crafting some insidious plot.

They got to the bathrooms just in time to see Sheila come out, dressed in jeans and a pretty yellow slicker. A couple of her teammates were with her. And sure enough, Nicole was lurking near the drinking fountain, looking like a bully.

"What's up, Nicole?" Geena called.

Nicole ignored her. She walked right up to Sheila. "I'm not going to let you get away with kicking my teammates," she said in a tough-girl voice.

"Ew, I'm scared." Sheila turned around and smiled at her friends.

"You should be!"

Sheila made an impatient gesture. "Stop whining, Nicole. Everyone knows you're just mad because your no-talent team lost."

Nicole gave Sheila a push. "*We* lost because *you* cheated!"

" 'We lost because you cheated,' " Sheila mocked.

Nicole raised her fists.

Sheila stepped forward, holding her fists up too.

Geena quickly moved between the two girls. "Hey, cool down."

"She kicked Fiona!" Nicole yelled.

"I know. She's a creep and she deserves a good right to the jaw," Geena said. "But remember what happened to that boy you beat up last week. The dentist bills were outrageous."

There was no boy, of course. Geena was just trying to distract Nicole until she had time to realize that a fistfight wasn't the best way to handle the situation.

"Let's get out of here," one of Sheila's friends said. "This isn't worth our time."

"Sure." Sheila slowly backed down the path toward the street, keeping her eyes on Nicole. "See you at school, lumpskull."

Nicole followed Sheila and her friends with her eyes.

Geena had to laugh. Nicole's anger was just so over-the-top. "Would you lighten up?" she asked.

"They only won because Sheila cheated," Nicole said.

Geena shrugged.

"Winning isn't any fun if you don't play by the rules," Naomi said in her best prissy voice.

That made Nicole smile. She gave Naomi a friendly shove. "That's what *you* think, lumpskull."

GEENA AND NICOLE WALKED OVER TO TOSCA'S together. Every Saturday, win or lose, Marina treated the Stars to ice cream. They were allowed to order anything they wanted, except for banana splits.

As the girls pushed their way inside the cozy ice cream parlor, Geena was hit with the smell of sweat and cinnamon. The place was packed. The Suns, the team Geena's brother Peter played on, were squashed in along the front windows. The Stars had a table near the back wall.

Nicole and Geena went directly to the counter to order. Geena was slightly chilly in her wet, muddy uniform, so she ordered a *hot* fudge sundae. Nicole chose a marshmallow parfait with chocolate ice cream.

As the girls left the counter, Rose motioned for them to take two seats near her and Jordan.

Jordan, Rose, and Nicole all went to the same school—Country Day Academy. Geena was the only Star who attended Sacred Heart, a Catholic school just outside Beachside.

"Where have you guys been?" Rose croaked. She was starting to lose her voice. Her napkin was already crumpled into the metal sundae dish in front of her.

Jordan was sipping a cup of hot chocolate.

Geena made a face as she slipped into her seat. "Nicole was beating up some girl from the Galaxy."

"Sheila McGarth." Nicole sat down, neatly sliding her napkin onto her lap.

Rose drew herself up. "Not Miss Vote-for-Me-I-Care?"

"Yeah. Her."

"Miss Vote-for-Me-I-Care?" Geena repeated, her tone puzzled.

Nicole made a face as if she'd just licked a lemon. "That's Sheila's slogan for student council."

"Student council!" Geena laughed. "So what's the story—is Sheila a total dweeb?"

Jordan and Rose slid looks at Nicole, who turned a delicate pink. Geena instantly knew she'd said something wrong.

"I'm running for student council too," Nicole said. She sat up straighter, her stiff spine showing that she was hurt.

"Oh . . . sorry." Geena touched Nicole's arm. "At *my* school, student government is dweeb central. What's it like at Country Day?"

Nicole took a deep breath and relaxed a little. "Actually, it's cool. Country Day is based on the idea that the school is *our* school—the students', I mean. So student council has a lot of power. We vote for a new council at the end of the school year so they can help make decisions over the summer."

"The reps get to help pick the lunchroom food," Jordan said. "They got us a salad bar last year."

"The council also has a say in what gym classes

are offered," Nicole said importantly. "Like, I could suggest that the school get rid of volleyball and have a soccer class instead."

"That's excellent," Geena said.

"Tell her about the phone," Rose croaked.

Nicole smiled. "You can run to be a member of the council, or you can try to get elected council president. The council president is, like, the most powerful kid in school. She even gets an office with a telephone! But competition is really stiff, and if you run for president and lose, you don't get a seat on the council."

Geena was beginning to understand why Nicole was interested in student government. "So are you going to be the council president next year?" she teased.

Nicole's face darkened. "It's either going to be me—or Sheila McGarth."

Aha, Geena thought. That explained why Nicole was so anxious to beat the Galaxy. Her rivalry with Sheila was bigger than just a soccer game.

"So what's your strategy?" Geena asked. "How are you going to beat her?"

"My dad told me people vote for candidates

they know," Nicole said. "So I plan to introduce myself to as many kids at school as I can. Plus, I want my posters plastered all over school. I'm going to be drawing posters every night after I finish my homework."

Geena made a face. "You're planning to make posters by hand?"

"So?"

"So, use a computer. It's faster."

Nicole groaned. "Yeah, but our computer at home is the worst. I've been nagging my dad to get me a graphics card and a new printer. He says he'll do it, but does he? No."

"Come over to my house," Geena offered. "Our computer is loaded. My dad gets all the newest stuff for his business, and he loves it when we use it."

Nicole grinned. "Thanks! That sounds great."

The wind picked up on Sunday and blew the rain clouds out of Beachside. Monday was partly cloudy, and Tuesday was bright and sunny without a cloud in the sky—the kind of spring day that made Tameka itch to be outside.

When the last bell finally rang at school that

afternoon, Tess, Tameka, and Yasmine raced each other to the corner of Wood and McAlpin, the place where Yasmine had to head in a different direction. As usual, Tess won.

"See you guys in a few minutes!" Tameka called without breaking stride. She kept running until she got to her front porch. She unlocked the door with a key she wore around her neck. Then she dashed up to her room, where she threw off her school clothes and yanked on her stuff for practice.

Mr. Thomas got home from work a few minutes later. He put on his sweats and drove with Tameka over to Tess's house.

Tess was waiting on her front steps. She popped up as soon as she saw the car.

"While I was changing, I got an idea about how we can show our team spirit," Tess said as she climbed in.

"Great. How?"

"Remember the friendship bracelets we made each other at summer camp last year?" Tess said. "We could make special ones for the team."

Tameka considered Tess's idea. "Sounds great," she decided. "We could wear the bracelets all the time. I love it!"

"Not so fast, girls," Mr. Thomas said. "AYSO has a rule against playing with jewelry on. Remember?"

"But those bracelets are made out of string. They wouldn't hurt anyone," Tess argued.

"Jewelry is jewelry," Mr. Thomas said as he pulled up in front of Yasmine's house and beeped his horn. "And rules are rules."

Tess made a face, sinking back into the seat.

Yasmine and her twin brother, Yago, walked out of their house. Yago was a member of the Suns. His team had practice at the same time as the Stars. The girls always let him sit in the front seat. That way they didn't have to sit next to him.

"Why do you look so grumpy?" Yasmine asked Tess as she opened the backseat door.

Tess wiggled over to the middle of the seat to make more room for her. "Because I can't think of a way for us to show our team spirit."

"I can't think of why the Stars would *have* team spirit," Yago commented.

Mr. Thomas shot him a warning look. "Hey."

"Sorry," Yago mumbled.

Yasmine ignored her brother. "Maybe we could wear special T-shirts or shorts," she suggested.

"That's stupid," Yago said. "You have to wear your uniforms to games."

"He's rude, but he's got a point," Tess said.

"How about matching baseball caps?" Yasmine suggested.

"I can't wear a baseball cap over my braids," Tameka said.

"Take them out," Yasmine suggested.

Tameka gave Yasmine a get-real look.

"It's not a great idea anyway," Tess put in. "I mean, who wants to play soccer in a hat? Especially a *baseball* cap?"

"Nobody, I guess," Yasmine admitted.

Mr. Thomas turned into the Beachside playing fields. The parking lot was already filling up. He pulled into a space near the back.

"Don't worry," Tess said as the girls hiked across the lot toward the field. "We'll think of *something*."

Tameka saw that most of the grass on the field had dried out. Only the areas in front of the goals were still covered with bare patches of rutted mud.

Marina looked tired as she trudged across the field toward the team. Tameka noticed that she was carrying her book bag in addition to her usual net bag of balls and equipment. The Stars' coach was a graduate student. Her first year of school was almost over. But before she could enjoy her summer of freedom, she had to write two long papers and take a test.

Practice began, and the team started a running drill. The air was humid, and Tameka was soon covered in a film of sweat. Her shirt was soaked an hour later when Marina told the girls to get into a circle to stretch out before going home. Tameka looked around at her equally sweaty teammates—and noticed that one was missing.

"Hey, Marina," she asked. "Where's Rose?"

"Rose had her tonsils out yesterday," Marina said. Her brown eyes were warm with sympathy. "She's not going to be able to play for the next couple of weeks."

Tameka had been six when her tonsils were removed. She still remembered how sore her throat had been—and how lonely she'd felt waiting until she was well enough to go back to school. Rose could definitely use some company.

"Can we visit her?" Tameka asked.

"Her mom said she'd like that," Marina said.

Tameka glanced up at her teammates. "Let's go over to Rose's tomorrow," she suggested. "We can meet in front of Tosca's at four-thirty."

Tess, Yaz, and most of the other Stars nodded.

Jordan shook her head. "I can't. I have orchestra practice until five."

"Geena and I should probably meet you guys at Rose's," Nicole added. "We have to do some work on Geena's computer right after school."

Tameka shrugged. "We'll see you there."

JUST DO IT, NICOLE TOLD HERSELF STERNLY.

Country Day had a rule. Before you could run for student council or council president, you had to get twenty-five kids to sign a petition supporting you. Each student could sign only one petition.

Most of the candidates asked all their friends for their signatures. But Nicole had decided that was too easy. She already knew her friends would vote for her. So she'd decided to use the petition as a way to convince *strangers* that she'd be the best council president.

She took a deep breath, adjusted the I'M RUNNING FOR STUDENT COUNCIL PRESIDENT button she'd pinned to her T-shirt, and then stepped out into the middle of the crowded Country Day hallway.

A couple of boys were heading straight for her. One was pale and short and was wearing a blue button-down. His friend was taller and darker and had bad skin.

Nicole didn't know the boys, and that was precisely why she picked them.

These guys look like losers, she reassured herself. *I bet nobody has even asked them to sign yet.*

But as the boys drew closer Nicole saw their gazes dart toward her clipboard. Their eyes met, and they smiled.

Uh-oh, Nicole thought. But she forced herself to step forward. "Hi! My name is Nicole Philips-Smith, and I was hoping you'd sign my petition so that I can run for student council president."

"I already signed," the dark, pimply boy announced.

Nicole made herself smile at the kid in the blue button-down. "How about you?"

Blue Button-down smiled slyly at Nicole. "Why should I sign your petition?"

"Because I can't run unless I get twenty-five signatures."

30

"Yeah, but what am I going to get out of it?"

Nicole shifted her weight impatiently. "What do you want?"

"A soda machine for the student lounge," the boy answered promptly.

Nicole snorted. "In case you've been sleeping through health class, soda isn't exactly nutritious. Ms. Richardson would never approve one."

Ms. Richardson was the principal of County Day. She was always making speeches about how a healthy mind started with a healthy body. She wasn't a big fan of junk food.

"If you can't get us a soda machine, then you're not the candidate for me." Blue Button-down nodded at his friend, and they pushed past Nicole.

Nicole let them go. Feeling discouraged, she took shelter against the wall, closed her eyes, and rubbed her forehead. Begging for signatures was giving her a headache. "Maybe being council president isn't worth this much embarrassment," she mumbled to herself.

"Nicole, what are you doing?"

Nicole opened her eyes and saw Jordan watching her.

Jordan was wearing a plaid jumper over a white blouse. A ribbon that matched her jumper was woven through her French braid. She was carrying her books and notebooks in a tidy stack.

Nicole held up her petition and made a face. "Collecting signatures."

Jordan took the clipboard and scanned the petition. "You already have twenty-one. That's not bad. You only need four more. And I haven't even signed yet."

Nicole watched as Jordan signed. Okay, so she wasn't a stranger, but Nicole was beyond caring. She hadn't realized how difficult it would be to convince people she didn't know that she was the right kid for council president.

"Rose wants to sign too," Jordan said as she handed the petition back to Nicole.

"Is she back already?"

"No. She told me last week. Maybe you should bring the petition with you when we go visit her after school."

"Good idea," Nicole agreed. "That would mean I'd only need two more signatures."

"Getting two signatures won't take long," Jordan said. "Ask that girl with black hair. She's in my class, and she's really nice."

Nicole looked where Jordan was pointing. A girl was ambling down the hall in their direction. She had an inch-high buzz cut and was wearing combat boots and black fingernail polish. Not exactly the type of kid Nicole imagined voting for her.

Still, Nicole didn't want to look snobby in front of Jordan. She stepped forward, blocking the girl's way. "Hi, I'm Nicole Philips-Smith. Would you please sign my petition for student council president?"

"Hmmm? Oh, sure." The girl scribbled her name, gave Jordan a quick wave, and continued down the hall.

"Thanks!" Nicole called after her.

"One more," Jordan said.

"Piece of cake." Nicole squared her shoulders, then approached a group of four boys who were sitting in a circle on the floor. To her amazement and delight, two agreed to sign her petition.

Nicole practically skipped back to where Jordan was waiting. "I've got twenty-five! I'm done. I don't even have to bug Rose this afternoon."

"Congratulations," Jordan said.

Nicole draped an arm over her teammate's shoulder. "Come on," she said. "We've still got ten minutes before lunch period is over. I'll buy you a chocolate milk."

Jordan and Nicole went down to the cafeteria and spent the next ten minutes sipping chocolate milk and talking about soccer. When the bell rang, Nicole headed upstairs for fifth-period French. She decided to make a pit stop before class. She pushed open the door of the bathroom.

Nicole stopped dead when she saw Sheila McGarth and Sheila's best friend, Rory Carver, sitting on the bathroom floor. They were hovering over a piece of paper.

At first Nicole thought they were working on a campaign poster. But then Rory sat back, and Nicole could see they were huddled around Sheila's petition. Nicole was surprised Sheila hadn't turned in her petition yet. She'd been wearing her VOTE FOR ME, I CARE button for at least a week. Then Nicole noticed something else: Rory was holding a fistful of pens. Each was a different color.

"What are you doing?" Nicole demanded.

Sheila looked up. When she saw Nicole, she smiled. "Collecting signatures."

"Collecting?" Nicole put one hand on her hip and glared at Sheila. "You mean you're *forging* the signatures you need."

Sheila shrugged. "Collecting, forging—same difference."

"If I tell Ms. Richardson, you'll get kicked out of the election."

A shadow of worry passed over Rory's face. But Sheila only smiled. Not a good sign.

"You don't want to tell Ms. Richardson," Sheila said.

"Why not?"

"Because if you do, I'll tell everyone in the school that you're a squealer. And nobody votes for squealers."

Nicole spun around and fled into the hallway. Sheila was right. As much as she wanted to tell, she couldn't. Nicole scurried into her French class just as the bell rang, feeling like a chump. Up until a few moments ago, she hadn't even considered the possibility that Sheila might actually cheat in the election. *If I want to win, I'm going to have to wise up,* Nicole told herself.

Nicole bit her lip as she stood over the Di Gregorios' printer. The machine let out a high-pitched whine and then began slowly rolling out a sheet of paper. Nicole impatiently grabbed the paper and flipped it over. A smile spread across her face.

Geena grinned at Nicole's obvious satisfaction with their afternoon's work.

NICOLE PHILIPS-SMITH FOR STUDENT COUNCIL PRESIDENT, the poster read. Geena had made the words as big as possible for maximum impact. The letters were solid and square—hard to miss. The middle of the poster showed Nicole's smiling face. Geena had done that by scanning Nicole's school picture into the computer.

"How's it look?" Geena leaned back in the chair in front of the computer, munching on a cookie she'd taken out of the family-size bag in front of her.

Nicole lifted her eyes from the paper and gave Geena a gleeful grin. "Perfect!"

"Then let's run fifty." Geena popped the rest of the cookie into her mouth and began moving the computer mouse across its pad. She clicked the mouse a few times, then pushed herself away from the computer. The printer whined back to life.

Geena glanced at her watch. "It's almost five. We're going to be late getting to Rose's."

Nicole nodded absently. She was still looking at the poster.

Geena found herself hoping that Nicole won the election. Her friend was going to be miserable—and miserable to be around—if she didn't.

GEENA AND NICOLE WAITED FOR THE PRINTER to finish spitting out the posters. Nicole carefully stashed the stack of them in her book bag. Geena turned off the computer, and the girls headed to Rose's.

At a corner near Geena's house, they waited a few minutes for city bus 51. They rode toward the lake and hopped off at Lake Shore Park, a narrow stretch of sand and grass that ran for miles along the lakefront. They started to walk in the direction of Rose's house.

Rose—and Nicole too—lived in a fancy subdivision called Estates on the Lake. Geena's own neighborhood was nice, but the houses at Estates were about twice as big. To Geena they looked overgrown, like the weeds that sprout alongside a highway. Still, Geena had to admit it would be nice to live so close to the water.

Now that it was almost June, the lakefront was starting to come back to life after the long winter lull. Seasonal businesses, like boat rentals and snack bars, were open again. The marina was filling up as people began taking their boats out of winter storage. But the breeze off the lake was chilly. Geena was glad she'd brought a jacket.

Up ahead, a couple of girls were kicking a soccer ball back and forth. Geena didn't pay much attention to them until Nicole grabbed her arm.

"That's Sheila," Nicole said.

Geena slid a glance toward her friend. Nicole's entire mood had changed. Her happy satisfaction was gone, and she was practically bristling with dislike. Geena could kind of understand. Nicole had told her how Sheila was cheating on the election.

"You're not going to beat her up, are you?" Geena teased, trying to lighten the mood.

"No." Nicole's lips were pressed together. Obviously she wasn't about to be jollied.

"Who's she with?"

"Rory—her best friend. You should recognize her. She plays on the Meteors."

Geena squinted at the girls in the distance. She recognized Sheila from Saturday's game. Today she had her beautiful curly hair tucked into a baseball cap. The girl with her had a slender frame and short dark hair with bangs. Geena didn't really recognize her. But she figured that if Rory was Sheila's best friend, she had to be a creep.

"Want to turn?" Geena suggested. "Couldn't we go up that street and avoid them?"

Nicole shook her head slightly. "I don't want Sheila to think I'm scared of her."

Geena shrugged. She was content to let Nicole call the shots. After all, this was her battle. *Sheila and Rory probably won't even notice us,* she thought.

But Sheila stopped the ball as soon as she recognized Nicole. "Look who it is!" she yelled to Rory. "A couple of losers from the Stars."

Geena felt Nicole stiffen beside her. *Uh-oh,* she thought. Nicole had a bad temper, and Sheila really seemed to know how to get under her skin.

Geena suspected that if she didn't get Nicole out of there soon, she'd be breaking up another fight.

"Ignore them," Geena whispered.

But Nicole was scowling at Sheila. "We're not losers," she said in a low, dangerous voice.

"The Stars?" Rory asked. "Isn't that the team you buried on Saturday?"

"Yeah. In six feet of mud!"

Rory laughed. "What do you expect? Any team with Nicole on it has to stink."

"Stink like a skunk!"

"Or a rotten egg."

"Or B.O."

That last comment had Rory sputtering with laughter.

"Oh, grow up," Geena muttered. Her little sister Naomi made better jokes than that. Even her four-year-old brother, Luca, did.

Geena could tell Sheila and Rory were having a good time teasing Nicole. Part of their fun was seeing her fly into a rage. If Nicole would just laugh off their stupid comments, they'd probably find someone else to pick on.

But Nicole didn't—or couldn't—ignore them.

Her face was red, and her hands were clenched into fists. "We would have won if you'd played by the rules!" she yelled. "The Stars are much better than your stupid team."

Sheila's eyes narrowed. She scowled and moved closer to Nicole. "Oh yeah?"

"Yeah!"

When Geena's little brothers and sisters acted this way, she gave them a time-out. But she knew Nicole wouldn't appreciate a suggestion that she go to her room until she was ready to play nicely.

"Can't you guys solve your problems without fighting?" Geena sounded like Mary Poppins, even to herself. But really! All this macho stuff was beyond dumb.

Geena was surprised when Sheila smiled at her. "Good idea," she said. "If you think you play soccer so well, Nicole, why don't you prove it?"

"Fine," Nicole said. "How about a little two-on-two right now?"

"Fine!"

Geena caught Nicole's eye. "Not fine," she said quietly. "We're on our way to visit Rose, remember? And besides, I don't want to play with *them*. Why waste the time?"

Nicole stared angrily at Geena. "If you don't want to play, leave!"

"I'm not leaving unless you come with me." Geena crossed her arms over her chest.

Nicole ripped off the spotless pink jacket she was wearing and tossed it onto the grass. She threw down her book bag a few feet away. "This will be my goal," she announced.

"We need two," Sheila protested.

"So make one." Nicole rolled her eyes, fed up.

Sheila pulled off her jacket. She used it and her baseball cap to mark the other goal.

Geena stood a few yards away. "Come on," she urged Nicole. "Let's just go."

"What's the matter with your friend?" Sheila called to Nicole. "Is she chicken?"

Geena was not exactly mortally wounded by Sheila's comment. But she was beginning to realize Nicole wasn't going anywhere until this was over. She couldn't drag Nicole to Rose's by the hair. And if Nicole was determined to get into some sort of fight to the death, Geena couldn't desert her.

Not that I'm going to be much help, Geena reminded herself. This was her first season playing soccer. And although she'd learned a lot, she still wasn't exactly a ninja warrior with cleats.

Still Geena hesitated. She hated to admit it, but a part of her was scared of Sheila, of her violence and unpredictability. Geena hated herself for being scared of some bully. After all, Nicole wasn't afraid—or was she? Maybe her tough-girl routine was just her way of hiding her fear.

Well, then, Geena could hide hers too.

"I'm not chicken," Geena said. "Let's play."

Nicole didn't run over and give Geena a thankful hug. In fact, she didn't even look Geena's way. She already had her eye glued to the ball.

So much for gratitude, Geena though. Then she told herself to pay attention to the game. It was not going to be easy.

Sheila gave the ball a vicious kick and immediately started running for Nicole's makeshift goal. Nicole was on her. But when she got too close, Sheila gave her a shove. Nicole landed on her backside. Sheila continued toward the goal.

Geena stopped running. "Are you okay?"

"Yes," Nicole said angrily. She scrambled to her feet.

Sheila dribbled the ball right into the goal. Then she stopped it and turned to grin at Nicole and Geena. "That makes one for us."

Geena glared at Sheila. "No fair! You can't just shove anyone who gets in your way. That's not how soccer is played."

"It is now." Sheila tucked the ball under her arm and headed back toward the middle of the field.

Rory greeted her with a sly high five.

Creeps! Geena thought. She was imagining how Sheila would look if she suddenly punched her right in the face. Not that Geena would ever do that—but it sure would feel good. *Now I know how Nicole must feel,* Geena thought.

Sheila put the ball down. Again she started to dribble forward. Rory still hadn't touched the ball, Geena noticed. Sheila wasn't just a bully, she was a ball hog.

Nicole ran after Sheila. She looked almost dainty as she batted at the ball, trying to get possession. But she could have been a gnat for all the attention Sheila was paying her. She plowed right on toward the goal, pushing Nicole out of the way whenever necessary. *If we want to beat this bully, we're going to have to play it her way,* Geena told herself.

Until then Geena had been hanging back, letting Nicole take control of the game. Now she ran toward Sheila and the ball—faster, faster. She was planning to ram into Sheila as hard as she could. To knock her right off her feet.

But at the last second Geena slowed down. She was scared of hurting Sheila. Even though she wanted to ram into her with the force of a tank, she ended up just nudging Sheila with her shoulder.

Still, Sheila was surprised. She moved slightly sideways. Geena reached out with her foot to take control of the ball.

Got it! Now turn it around and go, Geena thought.

As Geena dribbled, Sheila stayed right at her side. Geena looked her way. All she got was a quick glance at Sheila's furious face. But that was enough to tell her that taking on this human bulldozer was a mistake. Then Sheila slammed into her like a battering ram.

Geena took the impact on her shoulder. She stepped sideways to keep herself from falling.

Just as Geena was regaining her balance, Sheila came at her again. *Whomp!* Geena stumbled sideways. She wasn't sure where the ball was anymore—and she didn't care. All she wanted to do was get away from Sheila.

"Leave her alone, Sheila!" Nicole screamed.

Too late.

Sheila backed up again. Then, *WHOMP!* She ran into Geena as hard as she could.

Geena's feet somehow got tangled up in each other—or had she tripped over the ball? She really couldn't tell. But she fell heavily onto her side with her arm trapped under her. She heard a horrible crunch as she hit the ground. Then she felt something give way, followed by a pain so intense that for a moment her vision went black.

When she could see again, Geena gingerly sat up, clutching her right arm in her left. She was afraid to look at her upper arm. So she concentrated on her hand, trying to wiggle her fingers.

Nothing happened.

chapter 6

After Geena fell, Nicole pounded after Sheila. But even as she pushed herself to run faster, she knew it was hopeless. Sheila was too far ahead. Nicole was powerless to stop her from shooting the ball right into the goal. Again.

"Ha, ha!" Sheila said. "I told you, you stink."

Nicole gritted her teeth. Somehow they *had* to score. She didn't care what it took. She spun around—and noticed that Geena was still sitting on the grass. She was clutching her arm.

"Come on!" Nicole yelled. "Get up."

Geena shook her head. Her face was all scrunched up. "I don't want to play anymore," she said in a quivery voice.

"Is she crying?" Rory sounded disgusted. "What a baby!"

Crying? That worried Nicole. Geena wasn't the type to burst into tears over nothing.

"Come on," Sheila said to Rory. "Let's go. Cry-babies make me sick."

Nicole watched in disgust as Sheila and Rory started to jog down the beach. Then she hurried to Geena's side. "What's wrong?"

"I think my arm is broken." Geena sounded brave. But she was biting her lower lip so hard that it was turning white. "I can't move my fingers."

"I'd better get help."

"Call my dad at work." Geena recited the number. "Tell him to hurry."

"Got it." Nicole jumped to her feet and quickly looked around. The beach ran along one side of the park. On the other side were a road, another strip of grass, and then a row of houses with big front porches that faced the park and the water. This was Nicole's neighborhood. She scanned her memory, trying to think who lived nearby.

"I'm going to go over to that yellow house," she quickly decided. She pointed so that Geena would know which house she meant. It belonged to a dentist who had an office in the same building as her father's medical practice. Nicole had gone to a very boring party there once. "I'll be right back."

Geena nodded.

Nicole carefully crossed the road and then dashed across the grass on the far side. She ran up the front steps of the big house and rang the doorbell.

Please be home, please be home, she begged silently. She almost collapsed with relief when she saw a frail, grandmotherly-looking woman crossing the carpeted floor. Maybe the dentist's mother. She wore her hair pulled back in a scarf.

When the woman answered the door, Nicole quickly introduced herself and explained what had happened.

"Come in." The woman motioned Nicole into the hallway and showed her the phone. Nicole called Geena's dad, who promised to rush right over, and then she dashed back outside. The woman came out of the house and stood watching from her porch.

"Come back if you need more help," the woman called.

"I will!" Nicole ran back to the park. Geena was

still sitting where Nicole had left her. She'd stopped crying, but her face looked drawn and pale.

"I called your dad and told him where we are," Nicole reported.

"Thanks." Geena smiled weakly.

Nicole avoided looking at Geena's arm. She was scared that she might see bones sticking out. She felt guilty. Geena never would have gotten hurt if she hadn't been playing with Sheila—and Nicole had pretty much forced her into that.

"I guess we're not going to get to visit Rose," Geena said, her eyes on the road. Apparently, she was watching for her father's car.

"Guess not. Geena, I'm sorry."

"Don't apologize!" Geena's brown eyes were hard with anger. "Sheila did this."

Nicole felt a brief flash of outrage. *Someone should teach Sheila a lesson,* she thought.

Mr. Di Gregorio pulled up a few minutes later. He was a big man, and dark, with a bushy beard and intelligent eyes. He left his car running by the curb and quickly looked over Geena's arm.

"We'd better head to the emergency room," he said calmly. "Nicole, do you need a ride home?"

"No, I can walk from here."

Mr. Di Gregorio slipped an arm under Geena's legs and wrapped another around her back. He picked her up just like a baby and carried her to the car. Nicole ran ahead to open the passenger door.

Please be okay, Nicole thought as she watched Geena and Mr. Di Gregorio drive off.

"Hello?" said a high-pitched voice. Giggles followed.

Nicole stood in the middle of her room, holding her portable phone. She had to bite back a groan when she heard the little-kid voice. She didn't understand why Geena's parents let her younger brothers and sisters answer the phone. They weren't good at it.

"Luca, is that you?" Nicole asked impatiently.

"Yes." More giggles. "Who's this?"

"Geena's friend, Nicole. Let me talk to your sister."

"Which one?"

"Geena!" Geez, little kids could be dense sometimes.

Luca seemed to get the message. He dropped

the phone, and a couple of minutes later Geena picked up.

"Hello?"

"Hi! How's your arm?"

"Broken."

Nicole plopped down on her bed, bummed out by the bad news. "I don't believe it!"

"Believe it. I'm not allowed to play soccer until I get my cast off. And it isn't coming off for at least six weeks."

"But the season will be over by then! We only have a few games left."

"I know." Geena sounded sad, but resigned.

"Does it hurt?"

"It aches."

Nicole and Geena talked a few minutes more. But Nicole was having a hard time concentrating on their conversation. She kept telling herself that Sheila had broken Geena's arm. This time, she'd gone too far.

"I'm going to tell Fiona and Lacey!" Tameka yelled as she jumped out of her father's car on Thursday afternoon.

Tess got an impish smile on her face. "Not if I tell them first!" She began to race across the soccer field to where Fiona and Lacey were standing with Jordan and Sarah.

Tameka took off after Tess, with Yasmine right on her heels.

Mr. Thomas stayed in the car. He'd just gotten a call on his mobile phone, and he was deep in conversation about some business thing.

Tameka ran hard, but Tess reached the group of girls first.

"You guys. Guess what?" Tess was a little breathless.

Fiona was stretching out her thigh muscles by holding one cleated foot up behind her. She looked like a flamingo, standing on one leg that way. "What?"

"We thought of a way for us to show our team spirit," Tameka announced before Tess could beat her to it.

Lacey grinned lazily. "What did you great brains come up with this time?"

"Fingernail polish!" Yasmine announced triumphantly. "Glittery gold polish for the Stars."

Lacey looked down at her own nails, which

54

were painted baby blue. "I like it. Metallic tones are very hot this year."

But Fiona shook her head as she dropped one foot and grabbed the other. "Sorry, guys. I can't wear polish. My parents have a no-makeup rule."

"Nail polish isn't makeup," Tameka said.

Fiona shrugged. "Try telling my mother that."

"No thanks!" Tameka was a little afraid of Fiona's mom. She was super-strict.

Yasmine shot a frustrated look at Tess, who gave her a sympathetic pat on the back.

"We'll think of something," Tess said with determination.

Tameka nodded distractedly.

Nicole had arrived, and even from across the field, Tameka could tell that something was wrong. Nicole looked furious as she purposefully marched toward her teammates—more like a soldier going to war than a kid going to soccer practice.

Tameka nudged Tess. "Nicole looks the way she does when someone steals the ball from her."

"She's looked that way ever since Sheila broke Geena's arm," Jordan reported quietly.

Tameka spun around to face Jordan. "Sheila did what?" she asked.

"Didn't you know?" Jordan asked. "Sheila broke Geena's arm. Nicole can tell you about it. She was there."

"I was wondering why they never showed up at Rose's," Sarah said.

Nicole walked up to them.

"What happened to Geena?" Yasmine demanded.

Tameka was shocked when Nicole told the story of what had happened at the park. Sheila McGarth was definitely bad news.

"Sheila and Rory think they're hot stuff now," Nicole finished up. "Whenever they see me at school, they make noises like babies crying."

"As if they wouldn't cry if someone broke *their* arms!" Tameka exclaimed.

"Yeah, well, I didn't tell them that Geena's arm was broken," Nicole said. "I was worried they might be proud they had hurt her so badly. I've decided we've got to beat the Meteors on Saturday. Sheila keeps saying she can't wait to see Rory bury us. She's inviting all her creepy friends to our game."

"I'd like to help put Sheila in her place," Tameka replied.

"No joking!" Fiona said.

"I'm going to my aunt's wedding on Saturday, so I'm going to miss the game," Jordan said. "But I'll think good thoughts for you guys."

Tess sighed and shook her head sadly. "I hate to say this, but we may have a hard time Saturday."

Tameka looked at Tess. Where was that coming from? Tess was the most gung-ho Star. She took soccer seriously, and winning meant more to her than it did to anyone else on the team. She was a big believer in mental attitude. Hearing her even *hint* that the Stars might lose was unheard of.

"Call the police, you guys," Tameka said. "The Tess we know and love has been kidnapped by a body snatcher. This is obviously an impostor."

Tess rolled her eyes. "You've been watching too much TV. All I'm saying is this: The Meteors are a strong team."

"We're a strong team too," Yasmine said.

"Well, yeah. Usually. But we're not all going to be at the game," Tess pointed out. "Rose is still recovering from her operation. Jordan's going away. And Geena can't play. That leaves us with eight players on the field—one fewer than we usually have—and no substitutes. The odds are stacked against us, big-time."

Tameka couldn't deny that.

Nobody said anything for a moment. Then Nicole stamped her foot. "I don't care!" she said stubbornly. "We've got to beat them. No matter what it takes."

"All right, everybody," Marina shouted. "Let's get this practice started."

Tameka stole a glance at Tess. Nicole was famous for coming up with sneaky plans. Saturday's game would definitely be interesting.

NICOLE TRIED TO KEEP HER MIND ON STRETCH-
ing out, doing the dribbling drill, scrimmaging,
and running laps. But she was having a hard time
concentrating on practice.

One reason was that she missed Geena. Practice
wasn't the same without her overly enthusiastic
friend.

The other reason was that Nicole kept thinking about what Tess had said. Beating the Meteors on Saturday wouldn't be easy with the team
down three players. And if the Stars lost again,
Sheila and Rory would make Nicole's life miserable. Not a happy thought.

Especially since their teasing made Nicole look

like a loser at school. And nobody wanted a loser for student council president.

The only thing that would be worse than losing to the Meteors on Saturday would be losing to Sheila in the election.

Marina jogged up to Nicole after practice. "How's it going?"

"Okay."

"Where's Geena today? Do you know?"

Nicole raised her eyebrows. "Didn't Geena's parents call you?"

A worried look flitted over Marina's face. "No. Why? What happened?"

Nicole hesitated, allowing the fact that Marina didn't know about Geena's broken arm to sink in. She could tell her what had happened . . . but maybe it was better if Marina *didn't* know.

Playing with a cast was against AYSO rules. Which meant Marina would never even dream of letting Geena play. But if Marina didn't know about Geena's broken arm . . .

"Nicole," Marina asked, her tone a bit sharp. "Did something happen to Geena?"

"Yes." Nicole smiled her sweetest smile.

"Something wonderful! She, um, won an award at school. A . . . good-citizenship award. Her school had a special ceremony for the winners this afternoon. And that's why Geena couldn't come to practice. Nothing to worry about."

For just a second Marina looked doubtful.

Nicole told herself not to panic. She kept smiling.

Then Marina smiled back. "Well, that's terrific. I'll have to say congratulations to Geena at the game on Saturday."

"Good idea," Nicole replied. "She'll definitely be here!"

★

"Where's Naomi?" Nicole asked as she took a seat at the Di Gregorios' kitchen table.

Geena grinned. People only asked *that* when they were planning to do something bad. Geena had figured something was up when Nicole appeared at her house after soccer practice without calling first.

Actually, Geena had been napping when Nicole rang the doorbell. For some reason her broken arm was making her tired. Maybe because she hadn't slept well the night before. No matter what position she got into, the cast seemed to be in her way.

"Don't worry," Geena said. "The coast is clear. Naomi's at the grocery store with Mom. Do you want a soda or something?"

"May I have a glass of water?"

"Yes, you *may*." Geena made a face as she started pulling glasses out of a cabinet—with her left hand. Nicole was so formal all the time! "So what's the big secret?"

"I want you to play in Saturday's game against the Meteors," Nicole said.

Geena put a glass of water down in front of Nicole and slid into a chair at the table. She popped open a can of soda and gave Nicole a have-you-lost-your-mind? look.

"How could I do that?" Geena held up her cast. "Remember this?"

Nicole shrugged and took a ladylike sip of her water. "Marina doesn't know about your broken arm."

"Oops, that's right." Geena slurped the first sip out of the can. "Mom asked me to call her. But I fell asleep as soon as I got home from school."

Geena was starting to wish she'd done as her mother had asked. If she'd placed the call as she was supposed to, she wouldn't be getting dragged into one of Nicole's schemes now.

Not that Geena didn't feel sorry for Nicole. She did. Sheila was a beast. But Geena knew herself well enough to know that she wasn't very good at lying.

On the other hand, *playing* in the game on Saturday would be much more fun than watching from the sidelines.

"I'm glad you forgot to call her," Nicole was saying. "And you should *keep* forgetting."

"What if I do? Don't you think Marina will notice this big chunk of plaster?"

"I've got that figured out," Nicole said. "All we have to do is make sure you play goalkeeper. The goalkeeper's gloves and jersey will easily hide your cast."

Just talking about this plan was making Geena's palms sweat. "Playing with a cast is against AYSO rules," she pointed out.

"So is kicking people!" Nicole leaned toward Geena. "But Sheila got away with that!"

"Someone could get hurt," Geena said quietly.

Nicole flopped back in her chair and let out an exasperated sigh. "I don't care! I'm so sick of Sheila's gloating I can't even tell you. She's going to be at the game on Saturday, which means we *have* to win. This is the only way I can think to do it. We don't have a chance if we're down three players."

Geena hesitated.

"Come on, Geena," Nicole pleaded. "Don't forget that Sheila broke your arm."

How true. Geena glanced down at her bruised right hand poking out of her cast. It looked as if it had been tie-dyed black and blue. Now that she thought about it, Geena didn't really want Rory to win on Saturday, either. "Okay, I'll play," she agreed quietly.

"How are you feeling?" Nicole asked as they hung out at the field before the game.

"Like I'm going to barf," Geena replied.

Nicole laughed. But Geena wasn't really kidding. She hated lying. She'd already lied to her parents about her plans for the afternoon. And she still had a big one to tell.

Geena had come to Saturday's game wearing

a long-sleeved T-shirt and a pair of goalkeeper gloves Nicole had dug out of her closet. Even though the gloves were a few years old, they looked brand new. Nicole said she'd only used them once.

Aside from the fact that Geena's stomach was tied in knots, things seemed the same as they always did before a game.

Tess and Tameka were out on the field playing with a ball Tess had brought with her.

Eco-freak Amber was ambling around the field, picking up tiny pieces of litter.

Mr. Thomas was chatting with a few of the other parents.

Fiona, Lacey, and Sarah were gossiping about something—probably boys—with their heads close together.

The Madrigals had just arrived. Yago was helping Yasmine haul a five-gallon jug of water over to the sidelines.

Well, one thing was different, Geena admitted to herself. None of her family was there. Which wasn't surprising, considering the fact that they thought she was at the library.

Between Thursday afternoon and game time

on Saturday, Nicole had called every member of the Stars and let them in on the plan: Geena was going to play with her cast, and they were going to keep quiet about it. Geena wasn't really surprised when everyone agreed. She knew how hard it was to say no to Nicole.

Ever since she'd agreed to play, Geena had been thinking of reasons she should sit out. What if she accidentally hit someone in the face with her cast? She'd break their nose! What if her family—who would be coming to Peter's game later—arrived early and saw her on the field? This whole plan was nutty. And dangerous.

Nicole sat down and started to do a hamstring stretch. "I still think you should practice making some saves with your cast," she told Geena. "Those gloves don't fit perfectly over it, and you should be prepared."

"No way," Geena said firmly. "My arm already aches. I don't want to knock it around any more than I have to. Besides, you promised to keep the ball away from the goal."

"I'll try," Nicole said. "Just relax."

Geena nodded. But she couldn't relax. The game was going to start soon.

Staring across the field to where the Meteors had gathered around their bench, Geena could see Rory's dark head among the group of girls. *That's the enemy,* she reminded herself.

Geena watched as a group of three girls ran up to Rory. Her heart sank when she recognized Sheila and her friends from the Galaxy. They were patting Rory on the back. Geena could tell they were laughing, even though she was too far away to hear them.

"Sheila's over there," Geena told Nicole.

Nicole made a sour face as she stood up again. "The Galaxy played at noon. They won, of course."

Tess and Tameka ran over to join their teammates. "Marina's here," Tess reported.

Marina was smiling when she joined them, but Geena noticed that her eyes were red-rimmed. *She was probably up late studying,* Geena thought. She realized that Marina's fatigue might work to their advantage. Maybe their coach wouldn't be as eagle-eyed as usual.

"Hi, guys," Marina said as she put her bag down on the aluminum bench that had been set up on the sidelines. "We've got about ten minutes before the game starts. Let me give you the lineup. Then I want you to warm up."

"Ask her!" Nicole whispered in Geena's ear.

Geena took a deep breath. *One, two, three* . . . "Can I play goalkeeper today?" she blurted out.

"*May* I," Nicole said.

Geena stuck her tongue out at Nicole. "*May* I play goalkeeper? I haven't been in the goal in weeks."

"She just got a new pair of gloves and she wants to try them out," Nicole chimed in.

Marina gave Geena a surprised smile. "It's nice to hear you speaking up for what you want." She pulled the multicolored goalkeeper's jersey out of her net bag and tossed it to Geena. "Enjoy."

Geena caught the jersey with her left hand. She pulled it on, not paying much attention as Marina ran through the rest of the lineup.

"Let's see a few laps," Marina said.

Geena started to jog, falling into step next to Nicole.

"You did it!" Nicole beamed an enormous smile Geena's way.

"Big relief," Geena admitted. But in truth, she

was terrified. And she still thought Nicole's plan was nutty.

"Captains on the field!" the ref shouted.

Lacey and one of the Meteors hurried over to the ref for the coin toss.

Geena waited to find out which goal the Stars would have and then ran toward it.

"Have fun out there!" Marina hollered, clapping.

"Sure," Geena muttered to herself. "I'll have a great time as long as the ball stays on the other side of the field."

chapter 8

SHEILA AND HER FRIENDS SETTLED IN ON THE grass not far from the Meteors' bench, eating Popsicles they'd bought at the snack bar. Sheila threw her wrapper on the ground. Of course Amber trotted over, picked it up, and stuffed it into her pocket. Sheila and her friends thought that was pretty funny.

Geena watched the whole scene from the safety of her goal area. *Obnoxious litterbugs,* she thought.

The teams lined up. Geena noticed that Rory was playing left attacker. She felt good when she realized the Stars' front line was Tameka, Lacey, and Yasmine—all strong players. Maybe they really could keep the ball on the other side of the field.

The Meteors' center attacker took the kickoff, passing to Rory.

Rory easily picked up the pass, moving toward the Stars' goal. Geena was surprised by how well Rory controlled the ball. When the girls had been playing two-on-two in the park, Sheila hadn't let Rory touch the ball once. So Geena had assumed Rory wasn't a great player.

Bad assumption.

Now that Geena saw Rory in action, she vaguely remembered her from the other games the Stars had played against the Meteors. She was one of the best players on their team.

Rory ran fast—really fast—while maintaining perfect control of the ball. She whipped by Yasmine, quickly driving the ball about halfway to the Stars' goal.

Geena's heart started to pound wildly. This wasn't how it was supposed to happen. The ball was supposed to stay on the *Meteors'* side of the field.

"Get it away from her!" Geena screamed to her teammates.

Nicole charged Rory with twice her usual energy. Rory felt the pressure. She passed a real zinger back to the Meteors' center forward, who dribbled straight for the Stars' goal.

Geena watched her come, feeling as if she were about to be hit by an express train. *Keep your eyes on the ball,* she reminded herself. She bent her knees and tried to stay calm. She was so nervous her knees were quivering.

Playing goalkeeper always made her uptight. But today was worse than usual. Geena knew that each time the Meteors shot on goal, everyone—the ref, Marina, all the parents, Sheila—would be watching her. What if someone noticed her cast? As if keeping the ball out of the goal wasn't enough to worry about.

Amber got between the Meteor center attacker and the Stars' goal. The Meteor passed to her right, aiming for her right attacker.

Big mistake. Tess was playing left defender. The Meteor attacker trotted toward the ball, acting as if she had all the time in the world to take control of the pass. Tess intercepted. She hit the ball hard, lofting it way up into the air.

"All right!" Geena yelled.

Rory didn't miss a beat. She jumped up and trapped the ball with her chest. She used her knee to nudge the ball back to the ground, and she was off and running again. Straight at Geena.

This is bad, Geena told herself. *Very, very bad.* Nobody was between Rory and the goal.

Rory aimed and shot.

The ball headed toward the goal, spinning.

Don't panic, Geena coached herself. *It's coming a little bit to the left. Just move over a little and catch it. Don't worry about how much it hurts.*

Geena caught the ball against her belly, with both hands. *Oomph!* The impact forced all the air out of her.

"Nice save, Geena," she heard Marina shout.

You're doing fine so far, Geena told herself. *Now get rid of the ball.* She clutched the ball in her good arm as she jogged a few steps away from the net. Tess and Sarah, the defenders, were playing close to the goal. But Fiona, who was playing left midfielder, was open.

Geena tried to kick the ball to Fiona. The kick was short. But that was okay. Tess got the ball and whammed it all the way over the halfway line.

"Boo!" Sheila yelled.

"Don't let those losers beat you," one of Sheila's friends shouted to the Meteors.

Tess shot a surprised look over her shoulder. Geena shrugged. She'd never heard anyone booing at an AYSO game before. But she wasn't surprised that Sheila and her friends were rude enough to do it.

★

About twelve minutes into the first half, Sheila and her friends started chanting: "The Stars are los-ers, the Stars are los-ers, the Stars are los-ers," in low, singsong voices.

Nicole clenched her fists so hard that she could feel her fingernails cutting into her palms. *Ignore them,* she ordered herself. She tried to keep her mind on the game.

On the other side of the field, Fiona was battling one of the Meteors for control of the ball. It bounced out of bounds.

"Throw-in—Stars!" the ref announced.

Fiona quickly stepped over the touchline, brought the ball up, and tossed it to Amber. Amber got control and started to dribble forward. Nicole tried to stay even with her and open.

Now that the ball was closer to Nicole, Sheila

and her friends started to chant louder. "The Stars are los-ers, the Stars are los-ers."

One of the Meteors was racing toward Amber. "Behind you, Amber!" Fiona yelled.

Amber took the warning, passing quickly to Nicole. Too quickly. The ball scuttled across the grass yards ahead of Nicole.

"I got it!" Nicole yelled as she ran forward. She managed to get the ball under control just as a Meteor closed in from her left. *I've got to pass,* Nicole thought. She quickly sized up the situation.

"The Stars are los-ers."

Nicole gritted her teeth and forced herself to think. Yasmine and Lacey were both open. But Lacey was closer to the Meteors' goal, so Nicole sent the ball skittering in her direction.

Another poor pass. But the Meteors were miles away from Lacey. She had time to trap the ball and aim carefully. She kicked the ball toward the goal, high in the air.

The Meteor goalkeeper jumped for it. But her timing was off.

Poof. The ball landed softly in the net.

Shouts exploded from the little group of Stars parents and fans.

"Goal—Stars!" the ref called.

That made it Stars 1, Meteors zip.

"Yes!" Nicole yelled.

"Boo!" Sheila and her friends called.

"Nice one, Lace!" Yasmine gave her teammate a pat on the back.

"Thanks for the assist, Nicole!" Lacey said as the girls headed back to the halfway line. "Not bad for a 'los-er.' "

"My pleasure." And Nicole wasn't joking. She felt better than she had since Sheila cheated her way to the Galaxy victory the Saturday before. *My plan is working,* Nicole thought. If Geena hadn't played that day, the Stars would have had one less player on the field. They may have never gotten that goal.

A few seconds later the ref tooted her whistle for the substitution break. The Stars didn't have any subs to put in, but they headed over to the sidelines to see if Marina and Mr. Thomas had any advice.

Nicole fell into step with Geena. "How's it going in the goal?"

Geena sighed. "Well, nobody's noticed my cast yet."

"And they haven't *scored* yet," Nicole reminded her. "*That's* the important thing."

"Right."

"I like the way you're fighting out there," Marina said to the Stars as they gathered around her. "Good save early in the quarter, Geena."

"Thanks," Geena said softly.

Nicole winked at her. "Must be those new gloves."

"Nice goal, Lacey," Marina continued. "And good teamwork, Amber and Nicole. But you guys are letting your opponents pressure you too much. You're forgetting to aim your passes. Try to be more careful in the second quarter. Okay, same positions."

As the team trotted back onto the field, Nicole noticed the ref. She was standing over Sheila and her friends, gesturing for them to quiet down. Sheila looked annoyed. *All right,* Nicole thought. *Sheila's getting busted for booing!*

★

"*Another* great save, Geena," Mr. Thomas called.

Geena used her left hand to wipe the sweat from her forehead. She walked forward with the ball, scanning the field. Amber was open, and she kicked the ball in her direction.

Amber got control of the ball and then dribbled up the field.

Geena kept a close eye on the action. She knew the Meteors were capable of mounting a fast attack on the Stars' goal. They'd been doing just that over and over again all through the second half. Geena had responded with save after save.

With four minutes left in the game, the score remained Stars 1, Meteors 0.

The Meteors were tense. After fighting for almost an hour, they wanted a goal.

Well, too bad, Geena thought. She didn't have any intention of losing this game.

Amber passed forward to Tameka. She kicked the ball too hard, though. Tameka dashed for the ball, but a Meteor midfielder intercepted. She lost no time whamming the ball back into Star territory.

Rory got the pass. She and the entire Meteor front line came rushing toward the goal.

Geena kept her eye on the ball, which was spinning rapidly between Rory's cleats. Rory passed to a teammate who was in front of the goal. Geena moved left.

Wham! The Meteor player fired the ball like a bullet to the right corner of the goal. Geena dove right. At the last second she remembered her bad arm. She tried to protect herself by twisting around to land on her belly. But she hit the ground so hard that she grunted.

The ball was right in front of her face. Geena grabbed at it with both hands. The ball scuttled free, rolling out of the goal area in slo-mo. She crawled after it on her knees, surrounded by feet.

Geena reached again for the ball. A cleat whirled by just in front of her nose. She leaned back, grabbing blindly. She found the ball by feel and started to pull it toward her. Another foot. The kick missed the ball and connected with her right arm. *Crack!*

Geena felt a surge of pain like a jolt of electricity.

chapter 9

"GEENA, ARE YOU OKAY?" MARINA LOOKED ANX-ious, her brown eyes filled with concern.

Mr. Thomas was standing guard, keeping the rest of the team away from where Geena lay doubled over.

Geena gulped for air. Somehow the pain in her arm was making it difficult to breathe. "I—my arm is broken."

Nicole's father, a distinguished-looking doctor with graying hair and silver-framed glasses, moved closer.

"Can you sit up?" Dr. Philips asked kindly.

Geena tried. She could.

"Let's get a look." Nicole's dad pulled off the goalkeeper's gloves Geena was wearing.

Geena knew she should try to stop him. But how?

Dr. Philips sat back with a frown. "You're wearing a cast!"

Geena nodded, feeling miserable. She saw the look of surprise on Marina's face. Normally she would have felt bad about lying to her coach. But just then she was in too much pain to worry about it.

"Someone kicked my arm, which was already broken," Geena explained. "It really hurts."

"Is your mom or dad here?" Dr. Philips asked.

Geena shook her head.

"That should have clued me in that something funny was going on," Marina said as she gave Geena an I-can't-believe-you-pulled-this-stunt look.

Dr. Philips gently ran his fingers along the outside of Geena's cast. "Well, casts aren't designed to absorb major shocks like kicks," he said matter-of-factly. "This one is sporting a major crack. Chances are, Geena's arm is going to have to be reset. And her doctor will probably want a complete new series of X rays."

"I have a release," Marina said. "I could run her over to Beachside General."

Geena shook her head. She felt as if she'd caused enough trouble already. "That's okay. My mom and dad are at home. I can wait until one of them gets here."

Mr. Thomas stepped forward, holding out his mobile phone.

Marina made the call. She reached Mrs. Di Gregorio and quickly explained the situation. Then Marina and Dr. Philips helped Geena off the field. She sat on the team bench, cradling her arm.

By then, the shooting pains in Geena's arm had stopped. They were replaced with a constant throbbing. Tears welled up in Geena's eyes.

"Marina? I'm sorry."

Marina rubbed her back. "Don't worry. We'll talk about this later."

Mrs. Di Gregorio came trotting down the sidelines and spotted Geena. "Baby! What happened?"

"I'm okay, Mom."

Geena's mom had a quick conversation with

Dr. Philips. A couple of minutes later, Geena was tucked into her mother's car. They were heading for the hospital.

I knew Nicole's plan was dangerous, Geena thought as she stared moodily out the window. *But I never thought I'd be the one who ended up hurt.*

★

"Three minutes and fifty seconds remain on the clock," the ref hollered. "Let's finish up this game! Meteors get the kickoff."

A kickoff sounded pretty good to Nicole. At least they'd be starting at the halfway mark instead of right in front of the Stars' goal. That was especially important since Marina had refused to substitute a goalkeeper. The coach probably wanted her team to suffer some consequences for cheating.

Then again, Nicole thought, a kickoff didn't make sense. Kickoffs only happen after goals. "Why a kickoff?" she muttered to Yasmine as the girls moved into position.

Yasmine considered for a moment. "Maybe the Meteors' last shot went in."

"No way," Nicole said. That thought was too horrible to even consider.

Yasmine shrugged.

There's only one way to find out, Nicole told herself. "What's the score?" she shouted to the ref.

"One to one," the ref replied.

Nicole was stunned. How could the ref give the Meteors that goal? They'd sent Geena to the hospital on that play!

Well, maybe that wasn't fair. Truth be told, it was Nicole's fault that Geena got hurt. She'd talked Geena into playing with her cast. Just like she'd talked Geena into playing two-on-two with Sheila and Rory.

You're really a rotten friend, Nicole told herself.

The game started up again. Lacey kicked off to Yasmine.

Rory scrambled to intercept. She battled Yasmine for control; Yasmine's ponytail bobbed as she kicked the ball again and again.

Then Rory got in a kick that sent the ball out of Yasmine's reach. She dribbled toward the Stars' goal.

Nicole came forward to challenge Rory. But her heart wasn't in it. Rory faked left and streaked by Nicole on the right.

The Meteors had long since realized that Tess was one of the best Stars. Two players were covering her. That left Sarah, who was playing right defender, to protect the Stars' goal.

Nicole wasn't surprised when Rory shot right past Sarah and dribbled the ball straight into the goal. Without a goalkeeper, she didn't even have to risk shooting.

"Goal—Meteors!" the ref said.

"Way to go, Rory!" Sheila and her friends were going wild.

Nicole could imagine a scoreboard in her mind. Meteors 2, Stars 1. She could even picture a game clock with the time clicking down second by second. Probably not more than a minute was left in the game.

She glanced toward the sidelines, catching Sheila's gaze without meaning to. Sheila was smiling. Nicole could guess what she was thinking: *Nicole is a loser.*

This time Nicole wasn't in any mood to argue.

After the clock had run down and the Stars officially lost the game, the team headed to Tosca's as usual. Marina let the girls order and then called a team meeting. She talked about fair play and respecting rules.

Nicole was too numb with disappointment to pay much attention. In truth, she wasn't having any moral crisis about breaking the rules. But she had to admit that her plan had backfired. Geena had gotten hurt—and she felt bad about that. And the Stars had lost—she felt just as bad about that.

Her attempt to beat Sheila at her own game had been a complete waste.

★

"Did anyone have any brainstorms?" Tameka asked as she strolled through the mall with Lacey, Fiona, and Tess. They'd walked over from Tosca's. "Late-night inspirations? Anything?"

"Here's an idea. . . ." Tess's voice trailed off, her attention distracted by the window of her favorite game store. Tameka figured she was trying to tell if the store had any new books on chess strategy. When Tess wasn't knocking 'em out on the soccer field, she spent a fair amount of her free time checkmating other people's kings.

"Tess? Hello!" Fiona prompted. "You were talking; we were listening—could we get back to that?"

Tess didn't answer until they'd walked past the store. "All I wanted to say is that now might not be the best time for us to be showing our team spirit. Thanks to Nicole, the Stars have just gotten a reputation as a bunch of cheats."

Tameka knew all about why Tess didn't like Nicole. Tess thought Nicole was full of herself, bossy, and overdressed. Most of which was true. Okay, *all* of which was true.

But Tameka preferred to concentrate on Nicole's good qualities. Like her wicked sense of humor. And her intelligence. And the fact that she loved the Stars. Tameka knew Nicole hadn't meant to hurt the team by talking Geena into playing.

"We all knew what Nicole was planning and we didn't try to stop her, Tess," Tameka said. "If you think about it, we're all partly responsible for cheating."

Tess didn't have a comeback for that one.

Fiona motioned for them to follow her into Richie's, one of the big department stores. She led them to a makeup counter, where she started twisting up the lipstick testers.

"Don't blame Nicole." Lacey picked up a lipstick and smeared a brilliant red mark on the back of her hand. She held her hand out, admiring the color. "If that brat Sheila was bugging you every day, you might try something stupid too."

"I can't believe the way she was booing us!" Tameka said.

Tess leaned on Tameka's shoulder, bored.

"Maybe we should boo *her* next time," Fiona said. "We're playing the Galaxy next weekend."

Tess stuck her nose in the air. "Tess Adams does not boo her opponents," she said regally.

Fiona looked at Tameka.

Tameka grinned. Tess really could be too much sometimes.

"We'll fight back by finding the perfect way to show our team spirit," Tess declared.

"Did I miss something?" Lacey peered into the mirror and started to smooth the red lipstick on. "I thought you were against showing team spirit. And anyway, we don't have any ideas."

"Well, I'm about to get one." Tess straightened

up, closed her eyes, and put her fingers to her temples. She started to hum.

Tameka giggled. "What are you doing?"

"Waiting for inspiration."

"Well, hurry up," Lacey said. "You look weird. Someone might see you."

Tess opened her eyes and let her hands drop. She smiled with delight. "I got it. Socks!"

"Socks?" Fiona repeated.

"Socks," Tess said with certainty. "Socks with stars on them."

Lacey turned away from the mirror. The red lipstick made her look at least sixteen, although it didn't really go with her yellow soccer uniform. "Do they even make socks with stars on them?"

"Sure!" Tess replied. "For Christmas."

"It's June," Fiona reminded her.

Tess shrugged. "I'm sure there are some leftovers."

"Oh, sure," Fiona said. "I think I saw some Christmas socks right next to the bathing suits and suntan lotion."

"If you're done making stupid jokes, perhaps

we could go to the sock department and see what they have," Tess suggested.

The girls trooped across the sales floor. The walls of the sock department were crammed. Cotton socks. Wool socks. Businessmen's black socks. Multicolored socks.

"Look!" Tess grabbed a pair and waved them over her head. "I told you there'd be some leftovers!"

The socks really did look like something Santa Claus might have worn. They were knee-highs with a red background and a scattering of silver stars.

Lacey frowned. "We're going to wear those to a game? We'll look like elves."

Tess waved that away. "It will be fine if we all do it."

"How many pairs do they have?" Tameka asked.

Tess pawed through the pile. "Only five. But maybe they'll have more in the back." She trotted off to find a saleswoman, who went to check. A few minutes later the saleswoman came back and regretfully informed them that the store didn't have any secret reserves of the socks with stars.

Thank you, Tameka thought.

But Tess wasn't ready to give up. "I know! We could each wear one star sock and one normal one!"

Lacey flinched. "I don't think that's a good idea."

"Why not?"

"Well, we'd look like big-time fashion idiots," Fiona said. "And besides, these socks are twenty-two dollars a pair."

Tess double-checked the tag. "That *is* kind of a lot," she admitted.

Tameka saw her opportunity. She quickly started leading Tess out of the sock department. *I hope we think of a way to show our team spirit soon,* she thought. Otherwise, this could get very ugly.

chapter 10

NICOLE GOT HER FATHER TO GIVE HER A RIDE TO school on Monday morning. Sheila and Rory rode her bus, and she couldn't bear half an hour of their teasing and taunting.

Once her father had dropped her off, Nicole went straight to her locker. She couldn't decide if she should do her normal morning stuff—like hanging up campaign posters—or grab the books she needed and hide out in her homeroom until the bell rang.

Maybe she could avoid Sheila if she stayed out of the hallways. *Yeah, right. That's about as likely as Sheila being kidnapped by aliens. She won't miss this opportunity to give me a hard time about losing. She'll be looking for me.*

Nicole was just working her locker combination when someone tapped her on the shoulder. She turned around slowly, expecting to come face-to-face with Sheila's nasty smirk.

Instead she found Jordan. Dressed in black jeans and a lime-green T-shirt, Jordan looked more fashionable than usual. Only the green bow she'd used to hold back her glossy dark hair ruined the grown-up effect.

Nicole let out her breath in a whoosh. "Jordan! Hi. How was the wedding?"

"Fun. I got to see all my cousins. How was the game on Saturday?"

Nicole sighed dramatically. "The worst!" She gave a quick rundown of the day's awful events.

"How's Geena?" Jordan led the way down the hall toward the stairs. Both of the girls' homerooms were on the second floor.

"I talked to her yesterday, and she's fine," Nicole reported. "She had an *awful* time at the hospital. The doctors had to reset her arm. *Beaucoup* pain. But she's not in any trouble with her parents or anything. So that's good."

The stairwell door opened, and Rory and Sheila came out.

"Excuse me!" Nicole tried to push by them.

Nothing doing. Sheila closed the door. She leaned against it, blocking Nicole's way. "I'm really sorry the Stars lost on Saturday," she said sweetly.

Nicole shrugged. "Someone has to lose."

"So true," Sheila said. "But it takes a special team to lose even when they're *cheating*."

Rory and Sheila cracked up as they exchanged high fives.

Nicole was beginning to wish she had stayed home from school. She had a terrible stomachache. And looking at Sheila's face was making it worse.

Jordan took Nicole's hand and pulled her toward the next stairwell. "Ignore her," she said.

"Everyone tells me that! And I'm trying, believe me."

Nicole pushed open the door, and they went into the stairwell. Dozens—maybe even hundreds—of Sheila's campaign posters stared back at them. Sheila had put them up like VOTE-FOR-ME-I-CARE wallpaper.

Jordan started to laugh. "I guess ignoring Sheila isn't that easy," she admitted.

It wasn't.

Everywhere Nicole went at school that day, she saw kids munching on yummy-looking candy bars. Each one had a MCGARTH sticker pasted on it. Sheila had been passing them out.

Nicole fought back by spending the first half of her lunch hour hanging up the rest of her NICOLE PHILIPS-SMITH FOR STUDENT COUNCIL PRESIDENT posters along the main hallway. She decided to ask Geena to print out some more.

By the time Nicole slid into her usual table in the lunchroom, she was starving. But she forgot all about food when she realized that her friends Laura and Bridget were eating Sheila's candy bars.

"You guys! How could you?" Nicole moaned.

Laura, a slightly pudgy girl Nicole had known since kindergarten, shrugged. "They're free."

"If you want a candy bar, *I'll* buy you one," Nicole said.

"What's the big deal?" Laura took another bite.

"I don't want *my* friends eating *Sheila's* candy bars. It doesn't look good. It looks like you're supporting her."

Laura grinned. "Don't worry, I'm still voting for you."

"I should hope so!"

Bridget was a very thin, tall girl with the habit of wearing her riding boots and breeches to class. Nicole had known her since nursery school. "Do we have to talk about the election at lunch every day?" she asked, wrinkling her dinky nose.

Something about the way she said it made Nicole suspicious. "Who are you voting for, Bridge?"

Bridget squirmed. "I don't know!"

"You don't know?" Nicole exploded. *This has to be a nightmare,* she thought. *Even my friends aren't supporting me!*

Bridget looked up and met Nicole's fierce gaze. "I have a perfect right to vote for whomever I please."

Nicole felt like screaming. Whenever Bridget got defensive, she started to sound like an uptight English teacher.

"That's true," Nicole said with all the patience

she could muster. "So, how are you planning to exercise that right?"

"I told you. I don't know."

"If you please," Nicole said mockingly, "explain why you're hesitating to vote for me—one of your oldest friends in the whole wide world!"

Bridget paled a little. "I heard you were planning to do away with Pizza Fridays. And that's simply not a position I can support."

"Me neither." Laura crumpled up her candy wrapper. "I love pizza."

"Of course you do!" Nicole took a deep breath and tried to get her anger under control. "Everyone loves Pizza Friday. And any student council candidate who tried to get rid of it would lose big-time. Do you guys really think I'm that stupid?"

Laura and Bridget looked at each other.

"I guess not," Laura said.

"Thanks for the big vote of confidence. Who told you that total lie anyway?"

"Rory Carv—"

"Sheila's best friend," Nicole interrupted.

Bridget nodded. "I'm sorry, Nick. I never thought Rory would lie."

"It's okay," Nicole said with a sigh. She paused

long enough to unwrap her lunch. Today was not Pizza Friday, so she had brought a roast beef sandwich, a bag of baby carrots, and some cookies from home.

"Sheila has surprised me a few times too," Nicole admitted. "She's so good at this campaign stuff that she'll probably end up in Congress someday. Her posters are everywhere. She would probably win even if she didn't cheat."

"So then why does she?" Bridget asked.

Nicole shrugged, munching on a carrot.

"She told some kids in our science class she was going to do away with homework!" Bridget reported. "You'd have to be a real dork to believe that."

Nicole pointed a carrot at Bridget. "And what would you have to be to believe I was antipizza?"

Bridget gave Nicole an angry look. "I said I was sorry."

"I know, I know. I'm just grumpy because I'm going to lose to Sheila. Again. It's beginning to feel like a nasty habit."

Jordan had wandered up to the table. She didn't say anything. She just hovered nearby. Jordan had relaxed so much with the Stars that

Nicole had forgotten how shy she was around people she didn't know well.

"Hi, Jordan," Nicole said in her friendliest voice. "What's up?"

"I have to show you something," Jordan said in a barely audible whisper. "And you're not going to like it."

Nicole threw the rest of her lunch back in her bag and followed Jordan. Laura and Bridget tagged along.

"Look," Jordan whispered when they reached the main hallway.

Nicole was so surprised that her jaw actually dropped. Each and every one of her campaign posters—the ones she had just hung up—was now sporting a mustache.

"Who—" Bridget breathed.

"I saw Rory doing it," Jordan whispered.

There's a big surprise, Nicole thought. She stood staring at the defaced posters. The longer she stared, the less anger she felt. Something more productive was taking its place.

Slowly, calmly, Nicole began tearing the posters off the wall. "This time they've gone too far," she said quietly.

Jordan looked vaguely frightened. "What are you going to do?" she asked.

Nicole ripped down another poster. "I'm going to win."

★

"I'm glad you're not giving up," Geena told Nicole on the phone that evening. "But exactly *how* are you planning to beat Sheila?"

Nicole lay down on her bed and stared at the ceiling. "I don't know yet. Actually, I was hoping you'd have a suggestion."

"Well, no. Except . . ."

"Except what?"

"Except I don't think you should try to do it by cheating."

Nicole groaned. "If you're going to start lecturing me, I'm going to hang up. I'm not after a good-citizenship award here, Geena. I want to be elected council president, whatever it takes. I'll cheat if I have to. Definitely."

"This isn't a lecture." Geena's voice sounded as calm as ever. *She* never lost her temper. "It's just that . . . well, of all my friends, you're the best at making sneaky plans."

"Thanks."

"You're welcome. Except that it turns out Sheila is sneakier than you are. She could out-cheat you blindfolded. She's meaner than you ever dreamed of being. She's—"

"I get the idea!" Nicole interrupted.

"Good, because I want you to realize that if you try to outscheme Sheila, you're going to lose. If you want to win, you're going to have to try something else. Something Sheila isn't good at."

"Like what?"

"How about playing fair?"

"I tried that. She drew mustaches on my campaign posters and lied to my friends—who believed her! The jerks."

"I know. But look at what happened at the game on Saturday. We tried to cheat. And because of that, we lost. Who knows? Maybe if I had stayed off the field, the rest of you guys would have won."

"Maybe. Maybe not."

"All I'm saying is that Sheila sets herself up by breaking the rules all the time."

"Do you think I should tell on her? Go to the principal or something?"

"Would you vote for someone who went to the principal?"

"No chance."

"So . . . Think of something else."

Nicole groaned. "Sure. I'll get right on that. In the meantime, can I come over and print out some new campaign posters? Without mustaches?"

"*May* I," Geena teased. "Sure. But we might have to bribe Peter to get him off the computer. Dad just got one of those new super-speedy modems. Peter's been cruising the Web night and day."

"How about after soccer practice tomorrow?" Nicole asked.

"Sounds good," Geena agreed. "We can probably talk Peter into watching some cartoons on TV."

THE NEXT AFTERNOON GEENA AND NICOLE found Peter parked in front of the Di Gregorios' computer. He was still wearing his dirty cleats from soccer practice.

"Scram," Geena told her little brother. "It's my turn to use the computer."

"Says who?" Peter's eyes didn't move from the screen. He clicked the mouse rapidly, playing some online game that involved shooting down spaceships.

"Says me."

"Great. Then I'm staying." Click, click, click. *Vizpt.* A spaceship bit the dust. But then another one seemed to wage a massive counterattack.

There was an explosion at the front of the screen, which made Peter groan dramatically. He put his hands over his heart. "They got me."

Geena moved between Peter and the screen. "Go now, while you're dead."

"Or what?"

"Or I'll tell Dad what you did on Saturday night."

"I didn't do anything!"

"Peter, Naomi told me."

Reluctantly Peter slid out of his seat. "All right, all right, I'm going."

"Close the door," Geena ordered.

Peter slammed it on his way out.

Nicole grinned at Geena. "You're so lucky your brothers are younger than you are. I never could have gotten rid of Tyler or Nicholas that easily. What did Peter do?"

"Who knows? I made that up." Geena plopped down in the chair and closed out Peter's game.

Nicole dragged a chair across the room. "Pretty sneaky, Geena! Hey, stay online for a minute. I'll show you something cool." She leaned forward and typed in the address of a Web page.

The page loaded almost immediately. An aerial

shot of Country Day Academy scrolled onto the screen.

"Your school has its own home page?" Geena asked.

Nicole nodded. "All the computer classes helped design it," she said proudly. "We finally finished last week. Total last-minute. I mean, school's almost over. Everyone's completely excited about it."

She clicked the mouse a few times, and the graphics changed. Now the screen looked like a blackboard with writing on it.

"This is the link to my English class," Nicole explained. "That's our assignment for tonight."

Geena made a face. "I guess you can never say you lost your assignment."

"The teachers thought that too," Nicole said. "But now we just tell them that we lost the assignment—when our computers crashed."

Geena giggled. "What else is there?"

"Everything." Nicole sat back. "Clubs have their meeting schedules. The cafeteria posts its menus. We even have a special section for the student council elections, but it's pretty boring."

She clicked the mouse a few more times and

showed Geena what was on the election page. It wasn't much. Just a roster of the candidates, and an announcement that the election would be held Friday during homeroom.

"There's a link for your very own campaign page," Geena said. "Look—'Nicole-Philips-Smith.' That's you."

"I know. But it doesn't lead anywhere."

"You haven't put anything up?"

"No."

"Why not?"

Nicole shrugged. "I've been busy. And besides, it seems lame. I mean, one candidate loaded a list of what she'd do if she got elected. And Sheila put up her campaign poster. It's boring."

"It doesn't have to be," Geena said. "You could do whatever you wanted to jazz it up. Sound. Video. We could make a campaign commercial just as MTV-slick as the ones real politicians use."

"We could?"

Geena nodded. "My dad has every Web-publishing program known to humankind. Do you want to do it?"

"Absolutely! Sheila isn't doing anything half as cool!"

Nicole stayed at Geena's until dinnertime that evening. They spent hours surfing around to different sites on the Web to get ideas.

The coolest online commercials by far had video, so Nicole decided she definitely wanted that.

"It'll be a little hard to do, but so what?" Geena said. "Who has video of you?"

Nicole made a face. "This could be a problem. I don't think anyone does."

"Your parents don't tape your birthdays?"

Nicole shook her head. "They think it's tacky or something. But don't tell Fiona that. Her dad tapes *everything*."

Geena smiled. "He sure does. I bet he has a shot of you making a goal. We could use that with a slogan like 'Vote for a Real Winner.' I mean, if you want."

"I want, I want!" Nicole replied.

★

Fiona was munching on an apple when she opened her front door the following afternoon. She was wearing bike shorts, an oversize T-shirt, and no shoes. "Hi, guys. Come on in."

"Thanks for helping out," Nicole said as she stepped into the hallway.

"Sure."

Geena had never been to Fiona's house before, but she liked it immediately. The living room was full of dark wood and homemade quilts. A grand piano over in the corner was covered with pictures of Fiona and her parents.

"Nice house," Geena said.

"Thanks. Come upstairs and I'll show you my room. I got the tapes from my dad last night. They're already up there."

"You have a VCR in your bedroom?" Nicole asked.

"Yeah, my parents' old one. But I hardly ever use it."

Nicole rolled her eyes. "And people say *I'm* spoiled."

"You *are* spoiled," Fiona reassured her. She led the way up the curving wooden staircase to the second floor and opened the door of her bedroom.

The room had a gleaming wood floor and three big windows. But there were no rugs, curtains, bookcases, or stuffed animals.

"It's . . . nice." Geena couldn't help sounding uncertain.

Fiona laughed. "Kind of looks like I just moved in, doesn't it? I can't have a bunch of junk in here because it bothers my asthma. All my books and stuff are in the family room and den."

"Oh." Geena knew Fiona had bad allergies and asthma. Everyone on the Stars knew it—especially after Fiona didn't bring her inhaler to practice a few times and got into tons of trouble. But Geena hadn't realized that asthma equaled no stuffed animals. Oh well. Fiona wasn't making a big deal about it. Maybe she didn't mind.

The girls settled down in front of the TV, and Fiona popped in a tape. "Dad doesn't put dates or anything on these," she explained. "So we'll just have to keep looking until we find what we want."

Fiona hit Play on the remote. The VCR whirled to life. First it showed snow, and then an image appeared. The girls could see a pair of men's dress shoes walking across pavement.

"Those are Dad's shoes. He must not have realized the camera was on." Fiona hit Fast Forward. There was a wide shot of a soccer field, with girls in yellow uniforms spread across it.

"There we are!" Nicole said. "It looks like we're warming up before a game."

The camera zoomed in on Fiona. She was wearing a heavy sweatshirt under her Stars jersey.

"This one is too old," Nicole said. "The commercial will look weird if I'm all huddled up in a coat. Let's see if we can find the one from last week."

"No prob." Fiona tossed her apple core into the garbage can. She hit Stop, then Eject, and popped in a new tape.

The girls saw trees. And behind them, a bright blue sky. "It looks warmer already," Nicole said.

"There's Isabella!" Geena pointed at the image of her two-year-old sister, who was dragging her stuffed clown along the sidelines. "I remember this game—it was against the Asteroids."

"Right," Fiona said. "I had a goal."

Mr. Fagan had caught it on tape. There was Fiona, huffing and puffing but moving toward the Asteroids' goal with speed and determination. *Poof!* The ball hit the net, and Yasmine and Tess bounced into view, smiling and patting Fiona on the back.

"Did you score in that game?" Geena asked Nicole.

"Um . . ."

"No," Fiona said. "Jordan scored. Remember? She whammed it in from the halfway line."

Geena turned to Nicole, who was staring blankly at the screen. "When was the last time you had a goal?"

"In our last game against the Galaxy," Nicole said. "Off that penalty kick in the second quarter."

"Right!" Fiona said. She tried a few more tapes before she finally got the right one.

Nicole's goal wasn't there. The tape jumped directly from the ref calling the substitution break to a shot of Fiona gobbling down orange slices along the sidelines.

"If you're eating oranges, that's got to be half-time," Geena said.

"So where's the second quarter?" Nicole demanded.

Fiona shrugged. She rewound the tape and fast-forwarded through the beginning several times. No second quarter.

"I think I know what happened," Fiona finally said. "I sat out the second quarter. Daddy probably turned off the camera."

"He only tapes when you're on the field?" Nicole demanded.

"Well . . . pretty much," Fiona admitted reluctantly.

"You *are* spoiled."

Fiona stuck out her tongue.

"Come on, you guys," Geena said. "Let's think."

"I *am* thinking, and I *think* this is awful." Nicole was already deep into a sulk. "I can't make a campaign Web site out of one of *Fiona's* goals."

Geena felt bad for Nicole. She knew how important winning this election was to her. There had to be something they could do. Geena forced herself to sound cheerful. "We should still look through all of these tapes to be sure. Maybe Mr. Fagan *did* tape one of Nicole's goals."

"Geena, that will take hours! And the election is on Friday."

"What else can we do?" Geena asked.

"*Ow!*" Fiona was still watching the tape. She stopped it and hit Rewind.

"What?" Geena asked.

"I just saw that girl from the Galaxy whack me in the leg," Fiona said with a little laugh. "Nicole, you've definitely got to beat her. She's wicked. Watch this."

Fiona hit Play. There she was, on the screen, dribbling down the touchline. Sheila came into view, and you could actually see her pull back her foot and kick Fiona viciously in the knee, above the shin guard. You could tell Sheila wasn't even aiming for the ball. Fiona grabbed her knee in agony. Sheila dribbled toward the camera, grinning.

Geena was mesmerized. "Wow."

Fiona hit Rewind, and they watched it again.

"Wow," Geena repeated.

"More than wow." Nicole's sulky look was gone. She was beaming.

"Just watching that makes my leg hurt," Fiona said. "Why are you so happy?"

"Because I think I just won the election," Nicole said.

NICOLE GOT PERMISSION TO HAVE DINNER AT Geena's house that night. She ended up staying past her bedtime.

Geena and Nicole spent almost four hours in front of the computer. Editing the video and getting it uploaded onto Nicole's Web page turned out to be trickier than the girls had imagined. Peter, who was a miniature Web expert, came in to help.

"Let's see it one more time," Nicole said, stifling a yawn.

Geena typed a few commands. The video began running in a frame in the center of the screen. The whole thing was only about five seconds long. It started with Sheila's vicious kick, showed Fiona's agonized face, and froze on Sheila's nasty smile. The words DON'T VOTE FOR A BULLY scrolled across the screen, followed by PICK THE CANDIDATE WHO REALLY CARES. NICOLE PHILIPS-SMITH.

"Beautiful," Nicole said.

Geena's dad was watching from the doorway. He shook his head. "Are you girls sure this is the way you want the campaign to go? You're making your opponent seem pretty awful."

"She is pretty awful," Geena said.

"*Ugly* awful," Nicole said. "It's perfect. I just hope someone sees it before the election on Friday."

She stuck around long enough for Geena to print out a hundred more posters. If the high-tech approach didn't work, she'd have a low-tech fallback.

"Nicole!" Bridget clumped up to her the moment she walked into school on Thursday.

"Oh, hi, Bridge. Why don't you get some normal shoes? It's not like you're going riding during lunch or anything."

"I like my riding boots."

Nicole shrugged. "Walk with me to my locker.

I've got to hang up some more posters. I can't believe the election is tomorrow. I'm wired!"

"Forget about the posters!" Bridget said. "I saw your Web page."

"You saw it?"

"About a hundred times. I was looking for my math assignment late last night, after my parents went to bed—don't ask—and there it was. It's brilliant."

"Thanks!"

On the way upstairs, Nicole and Bridget passed the computer lab. A group of kids was clustered around one of the monitors. Nicole's commercial was on the screen!

Mr. Woodbury, the computer science teacher, spotted Nicole and gave her a thumbs-up. "Very high-tech stuff," he said. "I'm impressed."

"Thanks!"

Nicole and Bridget headed toward the stairs. The hallways were getting crowded. Homeroom was starting in about four minutes, and everyone was rushing to the lockers.

"Maybe I should ask him for extra credit," Nicole said as they started to climb.

"I think you're lucky Mr. Woodbury isn't mad," Bridget said. "That commercial is kind of mean."

Nicole shrugged. "Sheila's the one who's mean. I'm just letting everyone see her true self."

"Hey, it's the bully!" came a voice from lower down in the stairwell.

"Shut up, lumpskull! And get out of my way."

Nicole recognized Sheila's voice. For once, she didn't want to avoid her best enemy. She stopped, plastering herself against the wall so that people could pass, until Sheila climbed up to her. Rory was at Sheila's side, as usual.

"Hi, Sheila," Nicole said brightly. "I just wanted to say good luck tomorrow. Oh, and did you happen to see my new online commercial?"

"Yes!" Rory huffed. "And I don't think it was very—"

Sheila silenced Rory with a gesture. She shrugged, trying to act unconcerned. "I saw it. So?"

"So how did you like it?" Nicole was aware that things in the stairwell had gotten very quiet. Lots of kids had stopped to listen to her exchange with Sheila.

"Nice," Sheila said smoothly. "Of course, you realize nothing is stopping me from making a nasty little commercial of my own."

Nicole smiled right into Sheila's ratty little face. "Yes, there is," she said. "*I've* never kicked anyone during a game."

That wiped the smug look right off Sheila's face.

"Dogged!" one of the onlookers said.

Nicole practically floated into homeroom. She could hardly wait for the election the next day.

★

When Nicole arrived at practice on Thursday afternoon, the rest of the team immediately surrounded her. She felt like Winona Ryder or someone.

"I saw your commercial!" Yasmine announced with an enormous grin.

"We saw it at the school library," Tess put in.

Tameka nodded. "So cool."

Tameka, Tess, and Yasmine all went to Beachside Middle School, along with a bunch of the other Stars. "What made you guys look at the Country Day Web site?" Nicole asked.

"Fiona told us about what you and Geena were trying to do," Tameka explained. "She was won-

118

dering if you finished. We decided to look during lunch. It's completely awesome!"

"Only because Geena helped me," Nicole said. "She's a computer whiz."

"Don't forget that I gave you the video," Fiona said.

Nicole rolled her eyes, but she was really happy. "We couldn't have done it without you."

Amber shook her head at Fiona. "I can't believe you kept playing after getting kicked that hard."

Fiona shrugged. "I guess I was just focused on the game."

"Maybe we should send that tape to AYSO," Sarah suggested. "Sheila would probably get in trouble if they knew she was playing so rough."

Nicole shook her head. "I don't want to *tell* on Sheila. I want to *beat* her."

"You will," Tameka said.

"I'd vote for you if you were running at my school," Lacey said.

Nicole felt a bit uneasy with all the praise and attention. Not that she didn't like it.

She had never imagined that kids from other schools would look at her commercial. Of course, the Stars weren't just kids. They were her teammates. But still, Nicole couldn't help wondering who else had seen her handiwork.

★

"You're not eating," Laura told Nicole at lunch the next day.

"I know. I'm too nervous."

"Even for pizza?"

Nicole pushed her tray toward Laura. "Help yourself."

Laura eagerly picked up the floppy piece of pepperoni-and-mushroom and stuck the pointed tip in her mouth. She went back to reading *Fourteen* magazine.

Nicole twisted around for the hundredth time and looked for some sign of Ms. Richardson. The Country Day students had placed their votes for student council that morning in homeroom. The teachers had delivered the votes to the office, where the staff spent the morning counting them.

Classes had been torture for Nicole. Half of her couldn't wait for Ms. Richardson to announce the results. If Nicole won, Sheila would be humiliated. Delightful thought. But half of her was dreading the results. What if she lost? Total mortification.

Jordan slipped up to Nicole's table and sat down. Rose was with her. She looked skinnier, and still pale. But she was smiling—probably happy to be out of bed.

"Rose! You're back!" Nicole exclaimed.

"I had to come vote for you," Rose whispered in a scratchy voice.

"That's so sweet," Nicole said.

"Are you nervous?" Jordan asked, with a shy glance at Nicole's friends.

"Either that or I'm coming down with the flu," Nicole said. "I've been feeling sick to my stomach all day."

"The torture's almost over," Rose whispered. "Here she comes."

Ms. Richardson walked into the lunchroom. Nicole watched as the principal crossed to the stage, where a podium and microphone had been set up. She clicked up the stage steps, set the collection of papers she was holding on the podium, adjusted her glasses, and tapped the microphone.

"Good afternoon, people!" Ms. Richardson

said. "I'm here to introduce you to your new student council."

Laura reluctantly closed her magazine and gave the principal her undivided attention.

"Good luck," Bridget whispered.

Nicole crossed her fingers.

"The new council members are . . ." Ms. Richardson consulted her list. "Muriel Hurley."

There was a shriek from a table near the windows. Muriel, a slender African American girl with super-short hair, stood up and waved her hands in the air. Her friends cheered.

"Mary Armstrong," Ms. Richardson continued.

More whoops and hollers, this time from a table near the stage.

"Arthur Harrison, Marcia Cohen, Andy Barry . . ."

Nicole found herself tuning out as Ms. Richardson continued to read. She knew that the principal would announce the council president last.

Sheila was sitting on the other side of the cafeteria with Rory and a gang of their friends. Nicole thought she looked edgy.

Somehow Sheila felt Nicole's gaze. She jerked

her head around to stare at her opponent. Nicole quickly turned her attention back to the stage. Ms. Richardson said, "And the tenth member of our council will be Kenneth Vega."

Here it comes, Nicole thought.

Jordan shot Nicole an excited look.

Nicole bit her lip. She closed her eyes and prayed, *Please, please, please.* She tried to sit still, but she couldn't stop wiggling around in her chair.

Ms. Richardson cleared her throat. "And Country Day's new council president is . . ."

chapter 13

TAMEKA AND TESS TRAMPED UP THE LONG WALK-
way to Nicole's house on Friday night and rang
the doorbell.

A moment later Nicole flung open the door.
She was smiling and looked happier than Tameka
had ever seen her. Behind her, the house was blaz-
ing with light. Tameka could hear a hum of voices
in the living room, and she thought she recognized Yasmine's laugh.

"Welcome to my victory party!" Nicole said.

"Thanks." Tameka stepped forward and gave
her teammate a hug. "We brought brownies."

"Yummy." Nicole grinned. "Come on, Tess.
Come in!"

Inside, the party was rocking. All the Stars were there, plus a bunch of girls from Nicole's school. The TV was on in one room, the stereo was blaring in another, and the kitchen was full of food.

The girls had a dance contest. Then a cookout. Then Nicole's school friends took off. But the Stars settled in for the night. Nicole had invited them for a victory slumber party.

Tameka lay back in her sleeping bag and watched Lacey brush out Tess's long hair. She liked to play with Tess's hair too. Since she wore her own hair in tight little braids every day, she didn't get to mess around with it much. Of course, it was worth it, since she got to look like her hero, Cobi Jones.

"You know," Tameka mused, "we never did figure out a way to show our team spirit. And we're playing the Galaxy tomorrow. I bet they'll have their faces painted."

Tess groaned. "We've got to think of something. *Tonight.*"

Lacey gave her a little swat. "Don't move! I can't braid your hair if you insist on wiggling around."

Suddenly Tameka sat up straight. "You guys, I've got it!" she announced. "I know the perfect way for us to show our team spirit. Something even the Fagans won't mind if Fiona does."

★

"Nicole, you'll be our center attacker and team captain for the day," Marina said the next afternoon. The coach looked well rested. She'd finished the last of her work for school the day before. "Any questions?"

Marina paused for a moment, but nobody spoke up.

"Then I just have one more thing to say," Marina continued. "I've been involved with some great soccer teams over the years. My own AYSO teams when I was a kid. High school. College. But I have never, ever been involved with a team that had better *hairdos*!"

"All right!" Tameka said. She gave Tess a victorious look.

The entire team had been up late the night before. Now each and every one of them was sporting tight little braids just like Tameka's—in honor of Cobi Jones's dreads!

"I just have one question," Marina said.

"It's not against AYSO regs," Yasmine spoke up. "We checked."

"That's not what I was going to ask," Marina said. "What I want to know is, do you guys think you could braid my hair during halftime?"

Tameka grinned. "Not a problem!"

★

"I'm sorry you can't play," Nicole told Geena just before the game began.

Geena shrugged. "It's a bummer, but I'll live. Naomi says she's going to teach me how to cheer."

"Just be careful not to spell anything wrong," Nicole teased. "She'll tell on you."

Geena laughed. But then her expression grew more serious. "So, have you seen Sheila?"

"Yeah. But I'm trying not to pay much attention to her," Nicole said. The truth was, Nicole felt a bit nervous about playing against Sheila. She figured Sheila *had* to be mad about losing the election. What if she took her anger out on the field? What if she tried to hurt Nicole or another one of the Stars?

"Captains on the field!" the ref called.

Nicole flashed Geena what she hoped was a confident smile. "That's me," she said. "See you later."

"Have fun!"

Nicole ran onto the field, half expecting Sheila to be the Galaxy's captain for the day. She wasn't. Instead Nicole did the coin toss with a friendly-looking Japanese American girl. The Stars got the kickoff.

The teams took the field. Nervously Nicole scanned Galaxy territory, trying to see what position Sheila was playing. She wasn't in the front line. Or the midfield. She wasn't playing defender or goalkeeper.

So where is she? Nicole looked toward the Galaxy sidelines and spotted Sheila on the bench.

What a relief. Now Nicole could enjoy the game, at least until the first substitution break, without worrying about how Sheila was going to get revenge.

Nicole took the kickoff, passing to Sarah, who was playing left attacker. Sarah immediately lost the ball to a skillful Galaxy attacker. But Amber stole the ball back and passed forward to Nicole. The game was under way.

The Stars played well during the first quarter. So did the Galaxy. And both teams played clean.

Sheila stayed on the bench during the second quarter—which whizzed by. Nicole was surprised when the ref announced, "That's the half! Take ten."

The Stars hustled off the field. They only had a short break—and lots of braiding to do. Marina took a seat on the team's aluminum bench. The Stars circled around her.

"Let's do it!" Tameka's eyes sparkled.

Marina laughed as eleven pairs of hands went to work on her head at once. "Now *this* is what I call teamwork."

Nicole was making a braid just over one of Marina's ears when Fiona gave her a nudge in the ribs.

"Here comes your friend," Fiona said.

Nicole looked up and saw Sheila walking toward them. She had her eyes on the ground, and Nicole noticed that she wasn't wearing her cleats or shin guards. *That's weird,* Nicole thought. Playing without guards was against AYSO rules. Of course, Sheila wasn't exactly known for playing by the rules.

The Galaxy's coach, Rich, a young guy with a mop of curly blond hair, was walking with Sheila.

"What does she want?" Geena asked.

Nicole shrugged.

Rich walked up to the Stars' bench and smiled shyly. "Could I have everyone's attention?" he asked—unnecessarily because all the Stars were already staring at him and Sheila.

"Sure thing, Rich. What's up?" Marina *sounded* mature and intelligent. But she *looked* silly with her hair spouting out of her head like a half-braided fountain.

"Sheila has something she wants to say." Rich gave Sheila a significant look.

"I'm sorry if I played too rough and hurt any of you," Sheila said with her eyes glued to the ground. Her apology sounded more angry than sorry, and her usually loud voice was *very* quiet.

Nicole and Geena exchanges surprised looks. Where was *this* coming from? Everyone waited another moment for the rest of the apology, but it seemed that Sheila was done.

Rich cleared his throat. "I'm sorry too," he said. "I didn't realize Sheila was kicking other players until I saw it on the Internet. I thought I should check out the campaign video my whole team was talking about."

Most of the Stars turned to stare at Nicole. She felt just as surprised as they looked. The Galaxy was talking about her online commercial? And Rich had actually seen it!

"I want you all to know I don't approve of Sheila's behavior," Rich was saying. "I've benched her for today's game. And she's going to spend an hour picking litter off the playing fields."

Nicole looked at Sheila and thought she spotted tears in her eyes. *You're imagining things,* Nicole told herself. The idea of *Sheila* crying was ridiculous.

Still, Nicole almost felt sorry for Sheila. *Almost.*

"Come on, Sheila," Rich said. "Let's go."

Nicole watched as Rich and Sheila headed back across the field. Then she turned her attention to more important things. Only about five minutes were left in halftime. And she still had a lot of braiding to do.

Soccer Tips from AYSO

GOALKEEPING

The goalkeeper occupies a specific position on the soccer field, staying in that position while the ball is in play and defending the goal from the opponents' attack. The demands are unique; the pressure to perform perfectly each time the ball approaches is intense; and the skills and preparation required for the job are special.

The goalkeeper must always be in the ready position. She must constantly adjust her position as the angle of the ball changes. She must be focused at all times, able to communicate with her teammates loudly and clearly. And she must be able to consistently stop the ball from going past her and into the goal.

The goalkeeper has three main duties:

- Stop shots to prevent goals.
- Support the defense.
- Initiate and participate in the attack.

The goalkeeper must work on:

- Fitness—Flexibility, agility, strength, endurance, quickness, and coordination of movement are key physical characteristics.
- Psychological makeup—More than any other position on the field, the goalkeeper must be confident, courageous, and responsible.
- Technique—Catching, punching, deflecting, and diving are each challenging moves that require training and practice. A goalkeeper must work with her coach to learn these techniques.
- Tactical understanding—To anticipate the opponent and make quick and accurate decisions when initiating the attack, the goalkeeper must know how to read the field and make quick decisions based on the action.

Fun Games to Develop Reaction Time for Goalkeepers

Reaction time is critical to goalkeeping. An attack must be assessed and then defended against immediately. The faster the better. Here are two games to improve reaction time:

1. Sit on the ground with a ball in your hands. Using an instep kick, kick the ball high into the

air, then quickly stand and try to catch the ball before it hits the ground. As your reaction time gets better, don't kick the ball so high before you try to catch it.

2. Try this game with a friend. Have your partner stand about five feet in front of you with the ball in her hands. Do a front somersault. As you complete your tumble, have your friend toss it to you and try to catch it. As you get the hang of the game, have your friend toss the ball to the right or left so that you have to move farther to catch it.

AYSO Soccer Definitions

Attacker: A member of the team in control of the ball, who advances the ball and attempts to score a goal. Attackers need speed, power, good ball control, and accurate aim. Sometimes referred to as forward.

AYSO: American Youth Soccer Organization, a nationwide organization guided by five principles:

1. Everyone plays
2. Balanced teams
3. Open registration
4. Positive coaching
5. Good sportsmanship

Cleats: Projections on the soles of soccer shoes that provide support and a better grip on the soccer field.

Defender: The player whose primary duty is to prevent the opposing team from getting a good shot at the goal. Defenders need sufficient speed to cover opposing players, good tackling skills, and determination to win control of the ball.

Dribbling: Moving the ball along the ground by a series of short taps with one or both feet.

Goal: Scored when the entire ball crosses the line between the goalposts and underneath the crossbar.

Goalkeeper: The last line of defense. The goalkeeper is the only player who can use her hands during play within the penalty area.

Halfway line: A line that marks the middle of the field.

Halftime: A five- to ten-minute break in the middle of a game.

Midfielder: The player who supports the attack on the goal with accurate passes and hustles to get back to help the defense. Positioned in the middle of the field, she must have stamina for continuous running.

Open: A player who is not being marked or covered by a member of the opposing team is open.

Passing: Kicking the ball to a teammate.

Referee: An official who ensures the safety of all the players by enforcing the rules during a game.

Save: The prevention of an attempted goal, usually by the goalkeeper.

Scrimmage: A practice game.

Short-sided: A short-sided game is played with fewer than eleven players per team.

Substitution break: A quick break during which the coaches can put in new players and the players can grab a sip of water. Substitution breaks come at one-quarter and three-quarters of the way through a game.

Throw-in: When the ball crosses the touchline, it is thrown back onto the field by a member of the team that did not touch the ball last. The thrower must keep both feet on or behind the touchline and use both hands to throw the ball over her head.

Touchlines: Out-of-bounds lines that run along the long edges of the field.

Trapping: Gaining control of the ball by using feet, thighs, or chest.